LaST
BuLLET
CaLLS
it

ALSO BY AMIR GUTFREUND

Our Holocaust

The World a Moment Later

Takov and the Vicinity

LaST BuLLET CaLLS it

AMIR GUTFREUND

Translated by Yardenne Greenspan and Evan Fallenberg

amazon crossing

Text copyright © 2014 Amir Gutfreund
Translation copyright © 2017 Yardenne Greenspan and Evan Fallenberg
All rights reserved.

Previously published as הלדאו ונורב תדגא by ותיב-הרומז (*The Legend of Bruno and Adela*) in Israel in 2014. Translated from Hebrew by Yardenne Greenspan and Evan Fallenberg. First published in English by AmazonCrossing in 2017.

Published by AmazonCrossing, Seattle

www.apub.com

Amazon, the Amazon logo, and AmazonCrossing are trademarks of Amazon.com, Inc., or its affiliates.

ISBN-13: 9781477818046
ISBN-10: 1477818049

Cover design by David Drummond

Printed in the United States of America

For Dad and Ella

CHAPTER 1

AN EARLY MEETING

The police barrier glowed in the dark like a child who is happy for no good reason. An accident. Both cars were in a ditch: a jeep, its fender completely smashed; below it a small Fiat, hidden beneath the jeep's large body, as if searching for shelter from the pouring rain. An older police officer in a reflective safety vest motioned traffic on: "Move it, move it, nothing to see here." But people rolled down their windows, ignoring the rain. The cop waved them on, but there was no avoiding curious onlookers.

"Move, move on, nothing to see . . ."

For a moment the rain weakened, as if the storm had moved on in its great hovering journey over the Sharon region. The cop in the vest called out, "Zion, what about that coffee?" and thought about his wife. What was going to happen to her? The doctors wouldn't say.

A figure stepped out of the darkness. The cop shone his flashlight.

"Merlin? What are you doing here? Everyone's gone. I'm just handling traffic."

Superintendent Jonah Merlin studied the crushed cars. "Whoa," he muttered.

A black sports car pulled up next to the cops. The driver poked his head out the window and asked if it was the jeep's fault. Lightning flashed across the sky, and with one commanding finger Merlin signaled for the man to drive on. For a moment the driver hesitated, and then his head retreated back into the car. He drove away slowly, watching the scene.

"They won't let go," the cop sighed. "These accidents are all the same."

"It's instinct, Alex. People have to get a close look at a death that isn't their own. Instinct. You can't argue with this kind of thing."

Lightning cracked the sky again. Officer Alex and Superintendent Merlin stood waiting together for thunder that didn't come. The rain picked up again, huge drops now. The storm had made up its mind—it was here to stay awhile over the fields and roads.

"Move on, nothing to see," Alex rebuked another car that had slowed down. He gave Superintendent Merlin a suspicious look. "What are you doing here, anyway? There's no murder here. What has this got to do with you?"

"Actually, my car died, and I have to get to—"

The phone in Merlin's pocket chirped. He answered the call and walked away from Alex in the pouring rain.

"Thanks for getting back to me. Good. Listen, I tried to use Boardwalk Café coupons at your branch, but they told me—the shift manager said—that the coupons were only valid for weekdays, and . . ."

A car honked. Alex turned toward it. *What now?* He hoped his partner, Zion, would get back already with his coffee. He hoped this rain would disappear and take Superintendent Merlin with it.

Merlin appeared again from beyond the curtain of rain and said, "So, Alex, can you help me out? My car died, and I'm on my way to get a statement from someone near here. I saw your lights, and—"

"I can't, Jonah . . . really, I can't. I can maybe give you an umbrella."

"You're probably going to be here for another couple hours. I'll be back by then."

The veteran cop turned to the row of drivers with a fading voice. "Move on, move on, nothing to see . . ." He looked at the superintendent.

"So you really just happened to come here? It wasn't because of the screaming driver?"

"The screaming driver?"

"Well, you're not part of the investigation . . . I'm not sure I can . . . You're a demon, Merlin. A demon. Always were. Seriously, how did you know to come here?"

"My car died. My car—*that's* your demon."

"The paramedics pulled out two dead males from the Fiat," Alex explained. "But the jeep driver, who was seriously injured, wouldn't stop screaming: 'Murderers! Murderers!' Even after they put the oxygen mask over his mouth he kept on screaming. He said that a moment after the crash, before he even knew what was going on, some people came out of another car and told him they weren't there to help him, that he didn't deserve help, that he deserved to die for what he did. Just like that. And when another car pulled up, those same people told the new driver that everything was fine, that the ambulance was on its way. Just like that. Kept him from getting help. What do you have to say about that, Merlin?"

"How's the driver? Is he going to live?"

"He isn't doing well. Multiple injuries. But the way he screamed, like a beast!"

"So he said people came out of their car and purposely thwarted attempts to help him?"

"That's confidential, Jonah. I'm not supposed to tell you things like that."

"Did he say anything else?"

"It isn't a murder case yet, Jonah. Come on, this isn't your beat."

Superintendent Jonah Merlin stood there, silent and calm.

"He said that the guy who spoke to him was in a wheelchair," Alex said, unable to resist. "And that there was another guy, a giant. And another. Three of them."

"Okay . . . so what are the odds of you giving me a car?"

A great bolt of lightning lit up the sky, and within its illumination Officer Alex's stubborn face was severe and expressionless.

"Zion went to make coffee. That's the most you're going to get around here. I love you, Merlin, but that's it."

The wind blew the police barrier on its side, and Alex quickly stood it back up. When he looked up, Merlin was no longer there.

CHAPTER 2

A BODY IN SOUTH TEL AVIV

"Go slow," Merlin told the taxi driver. He didn't have an umbrella, and he didn't know which building it was. They'd said number twelve. The taxi's headlights cleared a path through the darkness. Merlin cracked open the window and heard the tires ripping through puddles. How could his car have broken down again?

The weather reports had announced a cold front from Europe. The winds mainly attacked in mornings and right before dark, like guerrillas. The drainage systems had been overwhelmed by the rain a while back. On the narrow, dark street, Merlin could see the flowing water advancing toward clogged drains.

End of the street. One-way.

"Go around the block," he told the driver.

Merlin opened the window halfway and stuck out his head hopefully. He heard the taxi driver grumble, and the rain made its way into the car, wetting his face.

"Right here, chief," he heard at last. It was the voice of the young officer whose head appeared through a gaping hole in the front wall of one of the buildings.

It was dry inside.

And there was a surprise—along with three young officers, he was also welcomed by Superintendent Eli Levy, who smiled at him like a hostess at a high-end restaurant.

"Hello, Jonah. To be clear, just because I'm here doesn't mean this is my case. I just dropped in."

"Hi, Eli. How's Limor? And this certainly *is* your case. You break it, you buy it."

Superintendent Levy sighed. "Forget about Limor right now." Then he raised a finger and warned, "You were late and I happened to be around, so they called me and I dropped in. I just dropped in . . ."

The forensics man, Efi Flint, who bore the predictable nickname Captain Flint, had heard enough of the conversation and motioned for them to follow him. They walked down three steps to the basement. The body of a young woman waited for them, lying on her side on the bare floor, her skirt pulled above her waist, one boot missing.

A floodlight on a tripod poured light over the scene, as if it were a film set.

Merlin crouched down carefully.

"Gunshot and strangulation," Flint told him. "Godzilla. Have you ever seen a one-handed strangling? This is it."

Merlin slowly got on his knees. He looked at the woman's face, at her clothes. He examined the area around her. There were two dark bullet holes in her blouse.

"The gunshots happened after she was strangled. Don't ask me why," said Flint.

"Designer clothes," Merlin noted. "Dorin Levy, Yehuda Etlin. The boot is a Bruno Magli." Taking a closer look at the woman's face, Merlin said, "Pretty."

"She was reported two hours ago. Some homeless guy," said Superintendent Levy. "No identification. She was cleaned out."

"Sex?"

Flint shook his head. "No apparent sexual assault, but a struggle. She went wild. Her fingernails are swarming with DNA."

"So what have we got here? Professional or amateur?"

"That's for the head of investigation to decide. And that's you, Merlin," said Superintendent Levy, glumly looking at the anonymous woman. "Half the junkies in town have left their footprints in this building. That's not going to make it any easier."

A thin layer of sand covered the bare floor, mixed with old oil stains and broken arabesques of shoe prints and bare footprints one on top of the other, losing their direction and swirling in a pattern around the dead woman. He also noticed some sweep marks. Slowly and carefully, he stood up and circled the body.

"Bried will decide who's in charge," Merlin said, his head tingling with a light headache. "Do you smell paint?"

"Paint?"

"Fresh paint. My headache can smell fresh paint in a second."

He pulled a tiny flashlight from his pocket and ran its beam across the walls. He found what he was looking for right away. Large, bold graffiti adorned the wall facing the street: "And I shed tears of happiness and helplessness."

"What is this?" Levy asked.

"This is an interesting case. Mine or yours? Should we flip for it?"

"You, you. It's yours. Limor is having a complicated pregnancy. I'm entering Code Limor until cigar time."

Merlin patted Superintendent Levy's back amiably, but clarified, "Like you said, we'll take it up with Bried. In the meantime, listen, the Internet on my cell phone doesn't work. Can you google this graffiti?"

Superintendent Levy smiled. "You mean you have no idea how to work the Internet." He began typing. "Just for you, Jonah, just for you. Hold on . . . no, no results for the phrase."

"Okay," said Merlin. "So in the meantime, why don't you tell your officers to go look for her car on the street."

"Her car?"

"I don't know what the story is here, but she's not the type to get murdered in a building in south Tel Aviv. In her league, this would happen at a five-star hotel or at her fancy home in Ramat HaSharon or someplace like that. If she's here, she either came by taxi or in her car. Have your officers go outside and look for her car. Or something."

———

Superintendent Eli Levy was happy.

They sat bent over, side by side, at the circumcision celebration of the son of one of the officers in their department, their chairs too close together, and the wall leaning inward toward the diners, forcing them to duck toward their plates and carry on their conversations from this pose. Across from them, outside the small square windows, the rain poured and Superintendent Merlin thought about the body, and the case that now officially belonged to him.

"Oh, Jonah, Jonah," Levy said, luxuriating in his moment. "What a show you put on for Bried. But nothing worked. I won. You're just bad, Jonah, you're bad at the most important thing—understanding Bried's brain."

Levy sucked on an olive, pulled the pit from his mouth, and presented it to Jonah. They both knew he was alluding to the size of Bried's brain.

They also knew that Levy was bound to inherit Bried's position one day, guaranteeing his bright future in the police force. Soon he would be made police commissioner, and then he would easily finesse the necessary maneuvers for the rank of police commander. Unlike Merlin's, Levy's path was paved. Unlike Merlin, he had a path.

Merlin protested. "There's so much DNA on that body that I can solve this case by tomorrow. Between you and me, the murderer might as well just turn himself in, because we've already got half of him under her fingernails."

Levy tried to sit back, but banged his head against the leaning wall.

"Ouch . . . fine, Merlin, fine. Enjoy your case. DNA and call it a day. Best of luck to you. I'm happy with the cases I got this week. Two thugs killed a homeless man on the beach. A husband murdered his wife in Ramat Gan and screamed that he did it. Open-and-shut cases. I'm happy."

"Say, did you get tickets to the festival already?" Merlin asked. "I only have two kids, but I need six tickets."

At that moment, a large man brought a microphone to his mouth and, with a screeching voice, announced the commencement of the round of toasts for the newborn. First up was Commander Menashe Bried. Their commander rose from his seat at the head of the long table. Superintendent Levy and Superintendent Merlin each grabbed an olive from the communal dish and began sucking on it.

"Listen," whispered Levy, "before I forget . . . last night, at home, I checked out that graffiti from the murder scene again. Still nothing. But I remembered something. There's this guy, some kind of journalist, he writes a weekly column for the local paper about graffiti around the city. Why don't you talk to him? What have you got to lose?"

"You have a name? A phone number?" Merlin whispered.

"What did you think, that I'd leave you to google on your own?" Levy said, giving his friend a piece of paper with a name and a number.

Rai Zitrin. *What kind of name was that?*

CHAPTER 3

RAI ZITRIN

Rai Zitrin grew up in the Bavli neighborhood, not far from the Yarkon River, within the pleasant and orderly collection of not-too-tall apartment buildings and lawns on which nobody plays. But from a young age he was attracted to the decrepit neighborhoods of south Tel Aviv, the intestinal alleys around Allenby Street, and the garages and warehouses of East Montefiore. At sixteen he rented an apartment with three friends on the edge of Jaffa, close to Bat Yam. From that point on he became an expert in the acrobatics of finding roommates with whom to share dilapidated rooms, alcohol, and cigarettes.

His parents named him Ephraim. He was named for his uncle who had been a paratrooper. Over the years he tried "Efi" and "Efri," and for a while even bravely carried his full name. Eventually, when a British friend struggled to pronounce his name, he registered the concealed "Rai" that had emerged from the foreign mouth and—bingo! "I'm Rai," he announced to the world. "Rai Zitrin."

Once a week he reported to the home of his parents in Bavli and tried to present them with his loot, like a sailor returning from faraway seas. But they were worried and weak. "What kind of work are you doing? Who are you hanging around with? Do you have a girlfriend?"

One evening, he tried to interest a veteran journalist thirty years his senior in the cultural character of the graffiti hidden around the city. Not those perfect artsy murals painted by talented artists with spray cans, but the simple scrawled statements: raging, funny, political, scathing, humiliating. The night began with a hesitant sexuality, but the more Rai talked about it, the hotter he got, and the journalist joined him in his sizzling. Two days later, the journalist called him and tentatively suggested he write a short column about the culture of these wall scribblings. A trial run. Not much money, no obligation. His offer included a frightened attempt to bribe Rai: "Don't tell anyone about what happened between us—I'm straight." Rai thought: *I think I'm straight, too.* He accepted the offer.

The column was successful and earned Rai an admiring audience. He slowly expanded his range of interest. Murals, protest installations, strange engravings, memorial signs, historical markings on houses, the remains of buildings swallowed within newer structures. A flood of e-mails to the newspaper invited Rai to come and examine sites, walls, signs. One poet wrote a poem about his column and performed it at readings: "I'm attracted to the wisdom of crumbling." Rai hated that. *The wisdom of crumbling?* He had never liked poetry or understood it. At the most, he liked the simple stuff, by Alterman, for instance. *The wisdom of crumbling? What the hell?*

Now there was a message about a cop looking for him. Cops didn't bother with the small things he did. A little hash. A blind eye to what his roommates stashed in their rooms. The message taken by the receptionist at the paper didn't mention the cop's tone of voice or whether he sounded threatening. Rai felt the note in his pocket, hoping it would tell him where he stood.

After eating well and buying cigarettes, he called the number.

"Superintendent Jonah Merlin?"

"Thanks for getting back to me. I might need your help."

For a moment, Rai thought he might get paid.

"How . . . how can I help?"

Merlin told him to meet him the next day for lunch. In public, in the middle of the day: no pressure.

Rai spent the night at a friend's house on Balfour Street, not far from the restaurant. The next morning the rain didn't let up. Dark clouds scudded above Tel Aviv.

He got there fifteen minutes early. Not a cheap place. He had wanted to be the one who waited, who received the cop, but the cop was already there, striding over to the door to shake his hand, giving him a quick once-over.

"Hello, Rai, thanks for coming. Come on, let's sit down. I'm starving."

Tense and discontented, he followed Merlin.

"So what is this about?"

"You look worried. Like I told you, I need help in your area of expertise, graffiti and whatnot."

"Uh-huh. And you also said you were from the Tel Aviv Central Unit and that you deal with murder investigations."

"You look worried. Have you murdered someone? Maybe you can close an open case for me?" Merlin wasn't smiling. For a second Rai actually felt under suspicion. Ambiguous circumstances—it would end with a prosecutor talking about events of some night, about something that never happened, vividly describing how Rai picked up a knife and stabbed, once, twice, twenty times. Blood everywhere.

"This is a great restaurant. I have some discount coupons, and my wife hates fish, so I thought, why not invite the graffiti expert? Have you been here before?"

Rai shook his head slowly. He was still tangled in the rope of terror fantasy. Murder in the first degree, life sentence. What did this guy really want from him? Rai only wrote about graffiti—he never actually made any. And anything like this restaurant was out of his league. If he was accepting money from his parents, then maybe he'd be coming here. They often dined in places where each setting had two different wineglasses. But he was meant for other things. Other places.

"I just want to pick your brain about some graffiti that might have something to do with a murder. But I swear, you've got nothing to be afraid of."

Rai smiled wanly.

"Let's order," said Merlin. "Then we can get to work."

Merlin ordered trout in lemon and butter. Seafood salad as an appetizer. A green salad and a glass of white wine. Rai also ordered the trout. Merlin urged him to get more.

"It's on me."

Rai ordered a cup of tea, and the waiter went off with their order.

"What does the phrase 'And I shed tears of happiness and helplessness' mean to you?"

"*That* has to do with the murder?" Rai said.

Merlin stared at him and didn't answer.

No journalist can make a living just off a newspaper column, and Rai wasn't even a journalist. He had a somewhat philosophical way of makings ends meet. Once, he had touched the bicep of a Palestinian construction worker and felt the hard, dense muscle, the true force of those whose strength was earned by physical labor. No mere pencil pusher who goes to the gym four times a week, his work completely divorced from his muscle. Rai had decided to get some real muscles, construction worker muscles.

He managed to get his name on the lists of building contractors and shipping companies. Sometimes they called Rai, and he got a workman's wages, but he had to work his ass off. Rai began to spend two or three days a week as a laborer, far removed from the image of the columnist, which had won him some renown. He wasn't big, but his body got hard and tight, just as he'd hoped, and the people who saw his ox-strong shoulders and broad back wondered how many hours a day he spent at the gym.

Merlin looked at him and seemed to be trying to fathom the secrets of the gonzo journalist's life.

He showed Rai some photographs just as the food came.

Rai looked at the spray-painted square red letters—"And I shed tears of happiness and helplessness"—and then looked at his fish. He was hungry. And nervous. The graffiti didn't mean anything to him.

"It's a stencil job. They didn't paint each letter separately. You make it at home, and then spraying takes about twenty seconds, and you've got some nice graffiti. I don't recognize the phrase, but I can think of something similar. For example, there was this guy who sprayed lines from David Avidan poems on buildings. It seems kind of similar. Maybe. What are you looking for?"

"I've got an unsolved murder on my hands."

"I'm sorry. I'm trying really hard, but I can't think of what else to say. Do you have any questions? Any leads you can tell me about? I want to help."

Merlin tore off a piece of bread from the basket. Ate some fish. Chewed his green salad. He seemed to have completely forgotten about his fellow diner. When he finally looked up from his food, his gaze was contemplative, distant.

"Oh . . . I'm sorry, Rai. Listen, I have to go check a lead, something I forgot. I'm leaving you enough money for the check and a tip. Use the coupons, too. Here's my card. I'll be in touch. I apologize, but I have to go."

Rai watched the superintendent as he hurried between the tables.

"And get some dessert," he called out as he left.

The discount coupons weren't valid for the lunch special, but the cash covered almost the entire cost, other than the tip. After a short argument and some smooth talking, Rai managed to leave the restaurant satiated, confused, and a little disappointed. It had been a fine meal, but he hadn't been useful. *Too bad.*

He walked slowly down Montefiore Street and reflected on how this was just one more day in his odd life. He thought he'd go look at a few back walls around the neighborhood before the sky began raging again.

CHAPTER 4

ELIYAHU SELFTER

We shall pay you back, Cain!
We shall take the souls of your young.

—Ze'ev Jabotinsky

"You see, Ephraim, just taking revenge wouldn't help me. What he did to your mother—that's exactly what I wanted to do to him. I promised myself he'd pay. Even if it took me my entire life—that's what was going to happen. But I had to think very carefully first. Get me to the other side of the road."

The enormous man tilted the wheelchair and rolled it gently along the crosswalk. When he pushed the chair onto the sidewalk across the street, he placed a gentle, supportive hand on the shoulder of the ancient man in the chair.

"To the right, Ephraim."

The chair swerved to the right.

"You see, Ephraim? Now we're going. But for years I just thought and thought and thought. Just thought. You should only fight a war after you've defined all your targets. Now the sword is leaving the sheath. If you had any brains in your head, I'd read you a poem now, Ephraim, and you'd finally realize what a great thing we're doing together. We'll have a meal at a restaurant today, all right? You can have whatever you want—just eat politely. Use a fork. We'll kill another one tomorrow. Watch out, there's a puddle."

It began to rain, large drops like elongated cheeks, and the giant pushed the wheelchair underneath a shop awning.

"Just a little rain, Ephraim, don't be afraid. We carry on! Let's go, Ephraim."

Dissatisfied but expressionless, the giant obeyed and moved them back into the rain. The old man in the chair and his escort moved slowly past people who had taken shelter, as if they were reviewing an honor guard.

"I was an ordinary child, Ephraim. The British ruled the land, and I saw the Landman brothers fight them. Evil versus evil. I've already told you plenty of times that I was meant to be born in a land of criminals called Poland, but in the middle of the big war, after the Nazis killed my father, the most wonderful man in the world, Dad and Bruno's admirers were able to smuggle my mother across the border. She didn't even know she was pregnant. Who could have even thought of pregnancy during those hard days? Watch out here, Ephraim."

The giant pushed the wheelchair carefully between exposed pipes. He bumped into some that blocked the way, lifted the wheelchair over the hurdle, and put it down gently. The old man reached out from his chair and slapped at the pile, scattering a few pipes.

"Nazis. They put them here so we can't get through."

Channeling the old man's rage, Ephraim took hold of some pipes and squashed them, slowly, one by one, until the old man said, "Enough," and the giant returned his grip to the chair's handles.

The two continued on their way through the rain.

"You're going to have to be a little patient, Ephraim. We're going tomorrow with Shimshon Krieker to another city, and we'll spend a few nights at a hotel. Only a few nights. That's the plan. We have to get there before and leave after. That's where you'll take your second revenge for what they did to your mother, Ephraim, and you'll be a hero. But you won't have your bed or your shower. We've practiced this, Ephraim, and now you have to be the best you can be, and not get angry because you don't have the same things you have at home. I promise you the beach and a restaurant, Ephraim. These are our great days, our final days. Shimshon will take us there, and Shimshon will bring us back. Don't worry. Everything will be back to normal in a few days. Just be patient. Avenge your mother, Ephraim, for what they did to her."

CHAPTER 5

A SECOND VISIT DOWNTOWN

This time, Merlin arrived at the murder scene in his own car. A working vehicle—a pleasure, even in the heavy rain.

He stepped out of the car and looked at the building. It stood out among the others, somehow more angular, more assertive. Now the building could add to its arrogance with the designation "Crime Scene."

He lingered at the entrance. There used to be a locksmith here. And a grocery store. Grocery stores usually have a back entrance for shipments. *An escape route?*

He looked around. Decay. Rubbish. Wreckage. Filth. The surrounding buildings looked hunched over, as if the fluid of life that erects walls had dripped and drained from them into the yards. *What kind of people lived here?*

Above, on the third floor, someone had put up a handsome embroidered curtain. An effort to beautify. Some people made an effort, even here. The same window also framed flowerpots, though in all the other windows, a wilderness of darkness. A unity of bleakness. He felt he ought to reach up and grab on to the pretty window, or else he'd grow weak and turn to stone.

He called Hadas.

"Hey, honey."

"Recharge me," he requested.

"I love you."

"More."

"You want to recharge or discharge? Because I have an urgent issue with the pair."

Since the day they were born, they called the twins "the pair." They were always up to something, the pair.

"Go."

The handsome embroidered curtain shifted a little. There was someone up there. Someone who could see the things that happened in the street. A witness, maybe. He'd go up there later, or he'd send Vadim, the young officer from his team.

"Turns out Omri joined the soccer club without asking," Hadas said. "He went to practice for two months straight and told them all kinds of stories about how he'd bring the money for registration. Now they're demanding we take care of it."

"That's it?"

"Ido messed up something with Omri's homework. In his note-book. Omri's response was to mess up Ido's notebook. We're talking about colored pens. They also punished the desk, the chairs, and the rug, but they didn't really mean to."

"I love you."

"You have a coupon for that. To be used tonight. I'll also have that lentil soup you love. Cilantro, cumin, and lots of lemon."

An ambulance passed. He loved that sound, the siren as it went by. Something, some large system, was functioning out there.

"I have to get back to work."

"Bye, love."

No one had walked by in the ten minutes he'd stood in the street. If it weren't for that curtain that had moved for a moment . . .

He took a deep breath. It was time to go inside.

Merlin moved aside some of the yellow tape that remained on the scene. He wondered where the officer appointed to guard the place was. Maybe Vadim let him go without asking.

He was already getting reports from Efi Flint's team: some helpful, some not. But as was his style, Merlin came back alone, letting his uninhibited stream of consciousness run loose. At some point, after all sorts of unresolved details had tortured him privately, they emerged to announce: *We're torturing you out in the open.* Merlin waited for this announcement, and then returned to the scene of the crime on his own. Sometimes this was the way he solved convoluted cases; other times, he roamed the scene for nothing, his soul playing dumb—*Me? I told you to come here?*

He pulled out his small notepad and shone a flashlight on the graffiti. The victim had yet to be identified, and the DNA she'd captured under her fingernails had yet to reveal a suspect. But Merlin wasn't concerned. Within two or three days the victim would have a name and would serve up many leads.

He moved the beam of light to where the floor met the wall. No shoe marks, unlike the rest of the room, which was riddled with the footprints of junkies, the homeless, and the illegal aliens. Someone had covered his tracks very carefully. Professionalism, or something else . . . the meticulousness of the amateur.

He remembered something that he had thought of at the restaurant with Rai Zitrin. There they were, those grooves in the layer of dirt and sand that covered the floor. Two parallel, thirty-centimeter-long grooves. Merlin remembered seeing Efi Flint's shoes stepping near those two lines, and that's how he'd noticed them. They didn't seem important at that moment, not significant, certainly not when only a few feet away lay a young, beautiful dead woman.

He thought of the victim, the killer, the act of murder. A murderer, any murderer, is a creature with limitations, with difficulties. Murderers carry equipment, operate tools, handle malfunctions. They leave marks.

Even dragons in fairy tales sometimes get stomachaches or ingrown toenails. They leave marks.

He let any thought, important or deviant, pass through his consciousness.

Let's go, thoughts, give me all you've got.

The pretty girl he saw in the morning. Yellow ankle boots. Very long legs, thighs exposed beneath a miniskirt, and red-and-green-checkered winter socks.

In the morning he'd spoken to Levy, who had already closed the case on the homeless man killed by two thugs on the beach.

"Piece of cake," Eli rejoiced.

"Really?"

"Ah, the pleasures of reconstruction. We went to the beach, at midday. For work, of course. I would have kicked off my shoes and gone to collect shells, but the two suspects were all over me: yelling, explaining, blaming each other and the establishment. And their lawyers. It didn't take them long to reach the 'I swear, my friend did it' phase. It's a shame they didn't kill that homeless guy on a yacht, a little deeper into the sea. Ah . . ."

"You're being insensitive. You're talking about someone who was killed."

"Yes, they took away his right to be a wasted junkie alcoholic and to mumble for a few months longer before he died of something else."

"To think that I know you and you're actually a pretty nice guy."

"Well, you know my opinions. I'm a cop, not a social worker. Any news on that girl of yours? She, on the other hand, should not have been murdered."

Should not have been murdered . . .

Murdered.

Here. In this black place. Flint's report left no doubt—this was not a case where the body had been dragged somewhere after the murder. Flint also determined that the victim had been waiting there. There were boot prints suggesting waiting, pacing.

He shone the light on the floor. He was searching for something that didn't appear in Flint's report. That was his drill: later he'd go back home and stare and halt the stream of his thoughts until something popped into his mind. He tried to practice this staring as he washed the dishes at home or did the laundry, but sometimes it happened in less convenient moments, even while he slept with Hadas. She got angry at first. "Come back to earth, Neil Armstrong." But with time, she got used to it. "I'll just wait here until you get back from your voyage."

The staring usually paid off. Details were revealed, as if someone had slid a knife along a mattress and all sorts of springs had burst out.

In the meantime, he had two grooves on the floor. He crouched down and stared at them. A wheelchair. As if a wheelchair had rolled along only thirty centimeters, landing from heaven and returning there right after.

He illuminated the letters again. "And I shed tears of happiness and helplessness."

He had to learn how to google things on his phone. It should be so easy.

———

Merlin wasn't supposed to be a police officer. He had been preparing to enroll at the university when his cousin Giora convinced him to try out for the force. Only for a few years, to save up. That would make going to school a lot more comfortable.

He passed the first battery of tests and interviews, and after a short course was added to a reserve force of patrol cops. A week later he was assigned to accompany a detective force that stormed an apartment in search of a dangerous fugitive. An old man opened the door and stood there, rubbing his eyes, stunned. His thin legs stuck out of a faded house robe as he asked in a trembling voice what was going on. He said he was the wanted man's father. He let the cops search the entire apartment, not demanding a warrant or any further explanation. As far as he was concerned, the cops were all right. It was his son who was causing trouble. Fifteen minutes later, orders were given to evacuate the apartment. The wanted man wasn't found, and neither was any incriminating or even interesting evidence. Downstairs, by the patrol vehicle, Merlin had remarked to the commander of the force that the father's robe hadn't been half-open like the robe of a man who just woke up.

The commander paused before saying, "What do you mean?"

"It might be nothing, sorry, but something didn't seem right. The tied robe. It looked like a show. Like he was waiting for us. He wasn't asleep."

They returned to the apartment. The old man broke immediately and pointed with a shaking hand toward the closet. There, behind a panel, his son was hiding.

Merlin was pulled from a career as a patrolman, meant to precede a university career, and joined the police investigative division.

He quickly became a detective. An outstanding detective, à la Sherlock Holmes. The one who notices slight deviations, catches obscure details. Police work entails a lot of micromanagement, organizing dry facts, and a brutal invasion into the depths of the minds of witnesses and suspects. There are tricks. There's luck. But that touch, the one that can flutter over the evidence and hearsay and summon the most important pieces, is almost always missing. A touch like Merlin's.

———

He glanced one last time at the graffiti. He understood.

If you put so much work into painting the letters, that means you're going to come back, right? You're planning more murders . . . this kind of snazzy production isn't a onetime thing.

You're going to come back, right?

CHAPTER 6

ZOE

She'd never seen such a large penis before. Well, it made sense; she was still young. She watched the man sleeping on the bed, naked, like a gigantic baby. Sprawled on his back and sighing. His huge hard-on riveted her. *What was he dreaming about?*

She sat on the windowsill and watched the Netanya beach. Still draped in dark, but the light emerging from the east was already rustling with color within the darkness. From the beginning, Julian told her he had no intention of trying anything with her, that he didn't sleep with young girls, and that in truth it had been years since he last cared about sex. She didn't believe him. She never believed any man, any person. If Martians landed on Earth, she wouldn't believe them, either. She only thought: *I have nowhere to sleep, and besides, whatever happens, happens. I'll be fine.* And Julian really was great. They moved from one pub to the next in the industrial zone, and he told her so much.

What could she remember now, in the morning? That in 1992 a container with thirty thousand colorful rubber ducks was lost at sea, and since then they've been floating, not a care in the world, surviving all storms, even swept peacefully to beaches, teaching oceanographers all sorts of things about ocean currents. Thanks to them, charts were being corrected. He also said there was no historical truth to the story of the Israelites leaving Egypt. Maybe there was something, but it had nothing to do with the Hebrew people. And that the name "penguin" used to belong to another bird that lived in the Northern Hemisphere, a bird that became extinct in the nineteenth century and was kind enough to relinquish its name. A good name for an animal is a valuable thing, and if such a great one as "penguin" suddenly became available, no one was about to let it sit on the shelf. And Julian talked about Cain and Abel. It bothered him that the Torah didn't say why Abel was murdered. It was kind of strange, but when he talked about the murder, you could tell he really cared. She promised herself to look at the Bible sometime and see for herself. *Could it really not say why Abel was murdered?* He knew lots of things, Julian, but he wasn't one of those guys who flaunted his knowledge, trying to hunt down girls. Actually, now that she thought about it, he stayed silent for quite a bit of time while she talked. Chattered nonstop. *That's just the way you are, Zoe. A moron.* He just tried to answer her questions and asked that she stay with him because he was lonely, never mind why. And scared, never mind of what.

Now he was dreaming, wrestling with something in his sleep, but still his penis was showing her that not everything was going badly in his dream. She hated dreams, because things were fucked up there, too. At three in the morning they were kicked out of the last pub, and he invited her to his hotel room. He made his promises, and she didn't believe them. But when they got to the room, he peed—not entirely inside the bowl—and fell into bed. He removed all his clothes and promised her it meant nothing, that he just wasn't able to sleep with any clothes on. For a moment she thought, *Here we go. You're going to suck some old paunchy man's dick. You screwed yourself over again, Zoe.* But Julian fell asleep in a second. He left her alone, totally awake. What did he tell her about Rabbi Akiva? *What was it? Never mind.* So much alcohol and two days without sleep—she had to rest, too. Had to. Had to. But it got away from her. Got away from her again.

Julian's hard-on went down a little. Maybe he had finished up what-ever he was doing in his dream. Maybe it was her in his arms. What did she care? In their dreams they can do whatever they want to her. Julian, diamond merchant from Belgium . . . *sounds like a cliché.* But after he had passed out, she checked his passports and other documents she found in his briefcase. His name really was Julian, Julian Levin. And if he did anything to her, she was going to the police, whom she hated. But he was sleeping like a noisy log, and his hard-on had wilted. Like hell he didn't care about sex. Now she was tired of the whole thing. He's fulfilled his potential, this guy. *Good-bye, Julian, you were sweet and taught me a lot about rubber ducks, and it's a shame I blabbed so much because if I'd managed to shut my mouth, I might have learned even more. And really, you were gentle and only wanted some company because you were lonely and scared. But it's morning now. You can stop being afraid. I'll find out for you why Abel was killed. Good-bye.*

Zoe kissed his forehead, jumped back a little in reaction to his short snort, and couldn't stop herself from slapping the flaccid penis mischie-vously. Then she left the room quietly. In the elevator she regretted not leaving a message on the mirror, written in red lipstick. *Whatever.*

And where was she going now? It was almost morning, and she couldn't sleep. Just couldn't.

———

She spent the whole day at the beach. Every fifteen minutes some idiot with Marlboro teeth who tried to hit on her interrupted her medita-tion. One sunny day in winter after so many days of rain, and all these types reemerged, men of the "very bad" and "please destroy" persuasion. Was there anything that would make them understand, if only for a moment, how unwelcome they were?

Her mother called. Twice. *You've got to try harder, Mom. I want hys-teria. I want five calls in a row, every five minutes; maybe then I'll believe*

27

you care about me. She glanced at her phone again. Two missed calls from "Mom cell." *Fine, Mom, you don't have to call five times. Three. Just three. Three in a row and you win, just like tic-tac-toe. Come on.*

In the meantime, she tried to find some shade where she could fall asleep, but every circle of shade was taken by a bunch of human creatures, and for people like her they left the sun, which decided that if it was going to come out once during this harsh winter, it had a right to roast them alive.

She left the beach and walked slowly by Julian's hotel. Squad car lights flickered around the entrance, and lots of people were crowded around, a few of them of the "very bad" persuasion, and others just regular, forgettable nobodies.

"What happened?"

"A tourist. They killed a tourist."

"A tourist?"

It took her five minutes to find out it was Julian. Her Julian. Oh God, they killed her Julian.

———

The police were determined to keep away all curiosity seekers, and she wasn't able to explain to them that she wasn't just a curious airhead, that she knew him and might be an important witness.

She couldn't make up her mind if she wanted to get involved in all this. *You've got a knack for trouble, Zoe. You're a world champion of trouble. What does this smell like to you, going over to those cops and announcing that you've spent the night with a guy who just got murdered? Oh, you didn't have sex? Yeah, right. And he told you about thirty thousand rubber ducks? Wow. And you haven't been at anything resembling school in three weeks, all under your mother's radar? Damn. Handcuffs, that's what they'll give you, and then, just like on all those police shows, they'll interrogate you without a lawyer, they won't let you sleep. Oh yeah, good one . . . won't let you sleep . . .*

She rubbed her eyes and decided to wait for the right moment, and then, as usual without thinking, she'd do something.

She spent about thirty minutes with the rest of the onlookers behind the yellow police tape. Nothing revved her engine; the right moment hadn't come yet. She thought of splitting, but stuck around anyway. It suited the hotel—named "Florina on the Beach"—this design with the yellow tape around the large flowerpots, the clear windows, the glimmering marble. And then, just as her mother called—*Not now, Mom*—a car parked and another cop emerged, and she saw right away that all the other cops treated him with respect. As if they'd been waiting for him. Not knowing how she managed to do it, Zoe approached him.

"I slept with him at the hotel last night. With Julian."

Slept. First lie, already.

What are you doing with this cop, Zoe, huh? True, it isn't every day that someone you were with ends up like this. They totally murdered that nice Julian. So you lost focus for a moment, Zoe, and now, because you're so tired, you'll blab to this cop, who'll get everything that happens on the bottom floor of the Hibiscus Club from you, all the details on your business with Gilly Miller, all the thefts from rich people's stores, everything.

———

Superintendent Jonah Merlin looks at the pretty girl with dark circles under her eyes. She sips hot cocoa with him in the hotel lobby. She gives him a strange testimony, like an encrypted message. He knows it's all lies, but he can't exactly identify them. He knows she isn't the murderer. Those thin, tanned, beautiful shoulders; the bewildered, submissive eyes; and the nervous spurts of laughter. *Not the murderer.* But her story, her dry narration of the final evening and night in the life of this now-dead body, isn't too helpful, either. Cain and Abel . . . the first murder. Is this a thread that would lead to that skull shattered with a blunt object, possibly a hammer, and to the blood dripping in all directions on the starched sheets, on which no sexual intercourse had taken place and on which none but the deceased had slept?

The pathologists had determined it was a very recent murder. The maintenance man who'd peeked through the half-open door found the victim a very short time after his murder, and he, the maintenance man, is now sitting in the hotel lobby, sobbing, while she, the girl who the night receptionist remembers slipping out at dawn, is talking his ear off in a tired, scared but teasing, sweet voice, never even hinting at the reason he was summoned from Tel Aviv to Netanya—the writing on the victim's bedroom wall: "All books aim at being authentic." Something that reminded one of the cops of the graffiti from Merlin's investigation in south Tel Aviv: "And I shed tears of happiness and helplessness." *Sometimes they aren't too dense, these Coastal District cops.*

The pretty girl, who says her name is Zoe Navon and has no ID—and claims to be eighteen but is lying—suddenly puts on a serious face, her upper lip trembling, her shoulders rebelling in a hard arc.

"So am I a suspect?"

He smiles. "What do you think? Do we have any reason to suspect you?"

He really should leave her here in the lobby with the hot cocoa. Thanks to her, they perhaps know something about the victim's final hours. But it isn't really important. She's just sitting here and lying, and pouting, and acting like a criminal caught after a shoot-out. And she was the one who approached him. She barely touches her cocoa, though she asked for whipped cream. Better for him to go to the hotel room, check on what the forensics people are up to, go through the dead man's things. But he wants to sit with this girl a little longer, to keep looking at her piercing eyes, such sweet lips, tanned shoulders, the collection of rings all on her left hand, each one probably meaningful in the complex world of Zoe Navon.

Five minutes, two questions, and he's out of here.

"But I was with him"—she's saying, her voice trembling—"and I don't have an alibi."

There's no need to take it easy on witnesses. One must slice them up, gain any advantage over them. But he's having a hard time using investigation standards on this girl. She might begin sobbing in his arms at any moment, her salty tears staining his shirt. Best to avoid that.

Besides, this isn't his case. What happens in Netanya, thank God, doesn't affect him. They'll question Ms. Zoe Navon. That's their business. They called him over because of the writing on the wall, and besides that writing, nothing here is his business.

"The lobby is an alibi."

"The lobby is an alibi?"

"The receptionist, the security cameras. You left early enough."

He smiles again. *What do young people see when an older man smiles at them? Is it even a pleasant sight?*

"So I'm not a suspect? Because I would never have hurt Julian. He was a sweetheart, and he didn't try anything. Who could ever want to murder him?"

"You're not a suspect."

Her shoulders loosen.

"Does the sentence 'And I shed tears of happiness and helplessness' mean anything to you?"

She's taken aback. She puts one foot up on her chair, heel against thigh.

"Of course. It's Bruno Schulz."

For the first time, she smiles at him.

———

She gets in the police car with a purr. Merlin closes her door and walks around to the other side. For a moment, beyond the windshield, he sees her image, her long shiny hair, and envies her. *I'm becoming an idiot.* He gets into the car and starts the engine. Then he turns his head and looks at her. Zoe reaches a finger over to the stereo. *The nerve.*

"What are you doing?"

She doesn't answer. The car fills with sounds from the album he was listening to on the way over. She whistles with enthusiasm.

"Assaf Amdursky's 'Dark Dream' . . . Superintendent Merlin, I'm impressed."

"Put your seat belt on."

Self-confidence flows through her, an amazing, strong current. Where is the scared, nervous girl who sat with him in the lobby?

That was the arrangement. The Coast cops would lend her to him for a while, he'd give her a ride to Tel Aviv in a real cop car, and she'd tell him everything she knows about the writing on the wall. But even before she starts talking, the engine is on, Amdursky is on, and suddenly she places two dainty hands over her eyes and leans back in her seat.

"Officer Merlin, sir?"

"What?"

"I'll tell you everything. Everything. I'm going to help the police . . ."

Pause. *What is she, on drugs or something?*

". . . but I suddenly feel my eyes closing. I can't hold on . . ."

Is she kidding?

Her head slowly droops. Zoe Navon is asleep.

CHAPTER 7

JONAH MERLIN'S TEAM

The busy work of the investigation moved like a long, convoluted line of ants—a misleading combination of tough confidence and total disorientation, crisscrossing. Where should he lead this investigation? What should he do with all those pages slipping out of the forensics department's printers and the reports of the police computer system?

Merlin had a small team, just two cops, outcasts from other departments whom someone in Human Resources decided to lump together with the terrible Superintendent Jonah Merlin—let the people who can't work together work together.

Subinspector Vadim Kelsitz was a young detective who'd made his reputation in the war against Russian gangs, and as a result of his overly enthusiastic use of the direct confrontation method, he got hurt and deflected from his career path. As a hothead who detested the office and thought paperwork was for women, he was sent to join Merlin's team. A temporary position, as far as Kelsitz was concerned.

"The best thing to do with an office desk is turn it over," he explained to Merlin when they first met.

Stereotypically, he had a good head for computers and a good relationship with the station's computer and web officer, Boris, whose office door had a sign that read "Microsoft, *Blat*"—a Russian expression of frustration and annoyance. Whenever Merlin had to become entangled in the web of the computer system, he sent Kelsitz instead.

Sometimes, during the long working hours, Kelsitz tried to explain the magic of his previous world to the desk people. "You have to understand, with gangs that traffic in women or drug kingpins, you have to earn their respect. So you have to see them privately. Not coming in like a cop with the law and the handcuffs when they have nothing on their side. You go privately. Then they give you respect. Get it? That's how I got hurt so bad. Blat."

Merlin tried to place Kelsitz in areas where he could be useful, and where his damage could be controlled. So he'd sent Kelsitz to check the street cameras, traffic light cameras, and business security cameras around the crime scene. He also sent him to that apartment with the dolled-up window, where a curtain was drawn over the first murder. Kelsitz returned and told Merlin that he'd found thirteen frightened Africans crowded in the apartment. He looked at them and they looked at him. One woman, the rest men. They were sure he was with the immigration authorities and that he'd come to put an end to their wondrous Israeli adventure.

"Me?" Kelsitz snorted. "Do something to immigrants? Report them? Me? Blat."

Born in Israel, Kelsitz's bitterness was fed by his parents' stories: how they were dropped in a miserable little town, in spite of what they'd been promised; how no one cared about their professional diplomas from their home country; how they were humiliated, insulted, ridiculed for every aspect of their culture.

Kelsitz's parents came to Israel from one of the small towns embraced by the Volga River, and the sanctity of the Volga in his memory led Kelsitz to scorn any body of water in the State of Israel. "You call this a river? Its length is half the Volga's width. You call this a stream? Back in the Volga, we don't even name a thing like that."

Kelsitz couldn't get any information from the apartment's occupants. He suggested that Merlin go back—privately. Merlin rejected the idea, but Kelsitz made a mental note to go back anyway. There was something there he didn't like. The one woman. Her expression. She wasn't scared, she even might have been glad to see a cop in the apartment. Kelsitz decided it was his business.

"I'll go back privately, but not now. What about Shulamit? Got any leads, Miss Shawarma?"

Advanced Staff Sergeant Major Shulamit Tal was the other cop on the team. She had doe eyes, a girlish ponytail, and contours that belied her forty years and four children. She spent her days in an ongoing divorce battle that had just turned seven, a process that became for a time an attempt at reconciliation but then returned with twice the zeal to the divorce track, only to deviate toward reconciliation once more. For a while, this attempt took place while living once again with her husband, Kobi, a period of time that led to the birth of baby Aviel and the rage levels of the current stage of the process. She talked about men as if she were a serial killer, but there was a drop of yearning for Kobi within the raging river of her discontent.

Tal was smart, able, and determined. She knew how to conduct an investigation without the kinds of mistakes you later pay for against defense lawyers. Mistakes of the "go privately" breed. Despite her dedication, on any given day at least one of her children had a cold, or a stomachache, or a doctor's appointment, so she was frequently late or absent from work. When she wasn't busy speaking to her lawyers on the phone or running to pick up one of her kids from school or kindergarten, you could find her quietly poring over her assignments, a shawarma in her hand.

Nothing about Tal's looks attested to her unlimited desire for grease-based street food. Merlin didn't enjoy seeing her sinking her perfect teeth into the meat. Once, devouring a shawarma, she grunted, "I haven't been with a man in seven years, and I'm not missing anything."

That remark, like others of hers, didn't quite coincide with the truth, and for people like Merlin, who knew every detail of her divorce saga, she'd add an apologetic caveat about the short time when Kobi returned to her life and she had the baby. "My mistake, may I burn in hell. An error in judgment. He seduced me, that jerk, with his new motorcycle."

Merlin tried to exercise his authority to delegate, but almost always forgot to follow through and didn't take much interest in the information collected by his team. He was an incorrigible individualist. He hated commanding and was truly bad at it. He survived officer training because his friend and fellow cadet Eli Levy took him under his wing, protected him, and risked disciplinary action for him. In the years after training they rose in rank almost side by side. But now, at this stage in their careers, the criteria for promotion were more about politics than crime-solving skills, and Levy's rise was about to accelerate while Merlin was beginning to lag behind. Most of the time he didn't care. Maybe his life would be better if he lost his job, or if he walked out on his own.

But in the meantime, he kept at his work, really making an effort. He admired and envied Levy's leadership skills. Once, like Levy, he took his team out to dinner, having watched Levy's group laughing in the station the next morning, full of energy and closer than ever. He gave the idea real thought and finally chose a high-end sushi restaurant, for which he had discount coupons. But Merlin's team-building effort failed. The next day Kelsitz told Boris, the computer guy, that warm sake wasn't really alcohol. Blat. And Tal told Merlin that she was never going to touch sushi again, and that people should decide if fish were alive or dead, no middle ground. *Besides, Japanese grill,* she'd said, *isn't really grill,* and he just had to trust her on that.

Merlin had a vague idea of trying an evening like that again, maybe bringing Hadas along this time. She'd know how to charm them. But he couldn't revive a second meeting out of the ruins of the first.

———

When Merlin drove up to the station with Zoe Navon, Kelsitz rushed out to meet him. The pathology report found that the one-handed strangling in the first murder was done with enormous, even awesome, force, and Kelsitz wanted to share the exotic details. When he saw the girl his face froze, like a man yearning to return to his previous career, the war on trafficking women.

"What's up, Vadim?" Merlin tried to remember what assignment he'd given him.

Kelsitz leaned into the window and showed him the report. He restrained himself once or twice when the girl, who looked as if she'd just woken up, brashly cut in on their conversation to comment. Finally, he fixed her with a look intended to chill her.

"A girl your age should be in school right now, yes?"

"Do you have recordings of your opinions? Because I'm interested in large-scale distribution."

Merlin told the two new rivals to break it off. He quickly briefed Kelsitz and left for his next assignment, which, to Kelsitz's great displeasure, included that girl.

Blat.

CHAPTER 8

THE FIRST VICTIM, RONIT HALEVY

It was a mistake; that much is clear. A mistake. And still, she came. *What is this place?* A deserted building. Empty. Dark. But this is where she was told to wait. She isn't scared, why should she be? All around her—and this is the amazing part—are evening sounds, a neighborhood. She could swear she heard a woman shouting, "Itzik, how do you want your eggs?" *What, some people come home from work to this place? This is where they live? Here?* Everything rusty, gray, black. The houses worn out and crumbling. *There are actual people who wake up here, say "Good morning" to the person beside them? Maybe even love each other here? Maybe.*

He'd sounded reliable on the phone. All right, he had some information about Claude. *But why here?* He asked for 20,000 shekels. No problem. But someone who demands 20,000 shekels for a few details about the man she's about to marry could set a meeting in the lobby of a hotel. Actually, he could do it without meeting at all. Bank transfer, using an unidentified account number. An e-mail from an unidentified server. What, is he afraid she'd go looking for him? She only wanted to know what they had on Claude.

Maybe they're afraid of Claude?

Afraid of Claude? Honey-bunny? Sweetcakes? Sugar-butt? Is it possible she has not realized what's hiding behind the mystery of her perfect man? He's the one who's so impressed by the fact that she was a sergeant in the army. Her foreign honey-bunny knows nothing about the army, about violence, toughness. She loves him—that's what counts. *So what is this information going to be? What are they going to say about him? Criminal past? Another woman? A genetic disease? Drugs? What?*

The man on the phone was calm. He knew she would come. He knew, *damn it*. Like sheep to slaughter. He recognized how easy it would be to make her submit, and they both knew he knew it. That's how it goes when you spend your entire life feeling guilty for no reason. He set humiliating terms for a successful businesswoman like her—and knew she would comply. Maybe he knows her? One of her acquaintances? Is it Gabriel? Benjamin? *No, impossible.* The people who know her don't know her at all.

And what does he have against Claude, anyway? Someone finally loves her and she loves him. No more of that endless zipper action, loving someone who doesn't love her, who loves another woman, who loves some other guy, who . . . *What was that? A rat? No, footsteps. No, it's a rat. Okay, the meeting's going to happen in a few minutes. A little talking in the dark.* Some information, and then she's out of here. She'll deal with whatever it is later.

Steps. Heavy steps.

What the voice on the phone didn't know was that she wasn't clueless. The private detective she hired is waiting in the building across the street. A guy who's done some jobs for her before. Reliable. If anything bad happens, he'll intervene. Maybe the guy on the phone thought that, with her upscale boutique and the expensive fabrics that pass through her hands every day, she'd be scared; she'd get here at the last minute, maybe even late. But she's been waiting for an hour. Waiting for him. They spoke on the phone five times before setting this meeting, and she was the one who set the tempo. She let him think she was scared. That she was spoiled. That she was dying to know what he had on Claude. But she wasn't born yesterday; she had worked hard to get where she'd gotten. The voice on the phone was mistaken if he had any ideas other than getting an envelope full of money in exchange for some real information. What does he even know about her? What does he know about what she's been through?

— — —

Her therapist said: "This is about your mother." *Great. Why don't you take your 600 shekels and tell me something I don't know?* But the therapist insisted, really worked that 600 shekels. Haute couture. "Something about guilt that has to do with your relationship with your mother."

You don't say.

Her mother, who lost her mind. Went completely nuts. Lots of women get a divorce, that's fine. Today even she, Ronit, realizes that her father was no great catch. Maybe her mother deserved a second chance. And lots of divorcées find God. That's fine too—*let her become religious.* But marrying a ninety-year-old rabbi? A mystic? Moving into his shit-hole barn in Safed? Only her mother could do that.

The voice on the phone had mentioned her mother's name. Her grandfather's, too. He said something kind of garbled. In all their previous conversations he'd spoken clearly. He sounded a little old, sure, maybe even elderly, but lucid. Confident. And then, in one conversation, his voice suddenly became muffled and he hung up. As if he were crying or something. And she's sure he said something about her grandfather, the famous Dr. Andreas Levin. That's what he called him. And what did he say about Dr. Levin's daughter, Sigal? That he'd seen her one time?

It was completely erased from her memory.

Too bad.

The voice on the phone had a moment of weakness. That would have been the right moment to pounce. To set terms. Just like in business. Or was it *she* who had had a moment of weakness?

What does she even know? Anyway, human relationships aren't an aspect of her life that she has any intention of improving. No need. She's good at business. She's good at romance. She's the best in fashion. The queen. That's it. That's how it goes. She was never taught to be nice to people. Even at family get-togethers, ever since she could remember. Like a bunch of people being held together by force, told "You're a family—get together," and then abandoned. Let them start smiling. Take an interest. Ask questions. But there's something disgusting in that family of hers. Not something she can put her finger on . . . a kind of stench . . .

What is this place? In this quiet, in this dark, she suddenly has more thoughts than she's had in thirty years. It's as if a vault has opened. Or a fist. Thoughts about her mother; her big, extended, disgusting family; their small, good family. Thoughts, thoughts. Five more minutes in this living grave and she'll burst with thoughts. Why does her mother live in that shit-hole of a barn? *Where's Keynan? Why was it sweet Iris who had to get sick? Why?*

In their nuclear family, they actually did have love. A small, close-knit organism. Mom, Dad, Keynan, Iris, and her. They didn't love their aunts and uncles, their cousins. Not because of anything they'd done . . . just because. Meeting them was repulsive, undesirable. Uncle Ari and his kids, Julian and Gili. Gili . . . she calls herself Gili now, but she used to be called Giselle. An awful girl. She had a pocketknife and would slice ants in two, right down the middle. And laugh. And there was their grandfather, the famous Dr. Andreas Levin. Ronit's mother hated her doctor-father. She never said why, never spoke about it. But within their small organism, they were a wonderful family. And then Iris got sick. Such a young girl. Everything fell apart after she died. Maybe her mother was entitled not to make it

41

through, to get a divorce. What does she even know about marriage? Her father remarried soon, as if nothing had happened. Then with his second wife, like rabbits—three kids, one after the other: boom, boom, boom. What does she even know? He must not have been a great catch to begin with, though now, with all this trouble, he was the only one who really applied himself, really tried to be useful. She invested the money, and her father invested all the time in the world into finding Keynan, who'd disappeared one day. America's a big place, and the police there don't get too worked up over an Israeli, an illegal immigrant, who vanishes. They were polite. They didn't tell the worried family that as far as they were concerned, their darling nobody could evaporate. But money talked. Her money. She dipped into her savings to find Keynan. Reduced her activity at the boutique. Adela understood. She said, "A brother's a brother." Adela even let her cry on her shoulder. With so many relatives and a fiancé, she ended up crying on the shoulder of her design partner at the boutique. Adela told her, "I have no siblings. I have nothing. Go, look for your brother. Take all the money you need. A brother's a brother."

A brother's a brother. In this big old world she has only one brother, whom she loved so much—and then, all at once he was gone, as if he actually did evaporate. As if the world had swallowed him whole. Her father tried. He flew over there, hired detectives. And her mother? That nutjob promised to pray for him. She said her new husband, the ninety-year-old righteous man—he'd know where Keynan was. He'd light a candle and pray, and then immediately be able to tell them where to look. *It's your child, crazy mother. You've already lost Iris.*

Adela tried to help, too. With all that weird style of hers, her eyes, which several customers said were like witch eyes, Adela tried so hard. She said, "Go, Ronit, I'll hold down the fort. What's more important than family?" She cut her maternity leave short and came back to work full-time, taking on all the responsibility with such tenderness. She really didn't have a family. Each day she had to find another solution for her baby. That baby . . . She'd never seen Adela with a man, and then one day she showed up at work and announced she was pregnant. She was thirty-four and she had to have a child.

"What do you mean *have to*?"

"Have to."

"But who's the father? Say something."

"Have to."

She never explained anything. That's how she was from the day they met at the Shenkar College of Design. Ronit had been insulted by something, or someone. She sat on a bench and cried. No one approached that "cold snob," that "talented bitch." Then suddenly this strange girl with the Slavic face who never spoke to anyone sat down next to her and put her arms around her. Without talking. Then she kissed Ronit's forehead softly.

They'd been together ever since. And now, with a baby to take care of and no family, that strange Adela cleared Ronit's schedule so she could find Keynan.

Ronit swore to herself that if things worked out and she found him, she'd fix him up with Adela, no matter what. So what if he's . . . whatever he is. They'd work it out. There had to be one couple in the world deserving of one another, two good people. Let them be happy.

But what's that got to do with reality? And where's Keynan? He finished his math matriculation when he was fifteen. He was destined for greatness. Why must everything be so cursed and disruptive in her family? She tried talking to her mother a few times. To understand. All her mother said was: "You won't understand. You won't understand what it's like to be on fire. Fire all the time. My righteous man, I can only live when I'm around him. When I'm around his white robe, I can breathe something other than coal and needles and uterine mucous. I serve him. I'm his slave. I love him, my righteous man. I can live two steps away from him, but if I take a third step, my throat fills up with black demon fur, with burial shrouds, hairy she-vampires, owls' claws inside my throat, my daughter."

Her mother's totally crazy.

But she still had those good, soft hands. *What, she uses those hands to caress his ninety-year-old naked body?* She still has pretty doe eyes and bouncy curls. It's her mother, who's always been kind and sweet, always made her feel safe and loved. Her and Keynan and Iris. A wonderful mother. *What made her lose it?* After Iris died, she had a few bad years, but that can't be it. *What was it, then?*

"You wouldn't understand."

Explain it to me, Mom.

Now she's there, in that shit-hole of a barn in Safed. Her daughter's a jet-setter, engaged to a finance man. She flies all over the world, creating clothes for the obscenely rich with her talented hands. Her daughter's a success story. *And what about you, Mom? Fine, get a divorce, become religious. But why a ninety-year-old rabbi? Ten years older than Grandpa the day he died. How?*

From the strange silence that creaks within the dark building she hears a multitude of gutters outside spewing water monotonously, like a band of tailors sewing all night long. Soft sighs from gutters in every direction. A muffled sound. *Why aren't there any other sounds here?*

Suddenly, within the dark of this deserted building, in this neighborhood of rat people and dying junkies, she's experiencing a strong flash, as if someone has just exploded a magnesium bomb. She can see with her own two eyes, as if it were in front of her, the picture, the one that was always sitting on that old bureau in her grandparents' living room. The family photo. The famous Dr. Levin with his wife and children. Serious, tense smiles. Formal clothing, but not upscale. Even in the old black-and-white photo you can tell that the stitching is amateurish. Miserable matching of the shirts and suits. The tie doesn't make any sense and is too short. But a family, nevertheless. The two children, Ari and Sigal. Her mother, sixteen years old, maybe a little older. A warm, good photo, in spite of the official air.

And that picture—*who knows where it is today, what drawer it's crumpled in, or what trash can*—suddenly appears before her. She can see Dr. Levin, her grandfather. His hand is resting heavily on Mom's shoulder, his daughter's shoulder. *How can she lie to herself?* That's the strongest thing she sees.

His hand. Heavy. On her mother's shoulder . . .

Mom?

Footsteps.

Mom?

CHAPTER 9

WE SHALL PAY YOU BACK, CAIN

Here, Ephraim, this is where she lives, that lady. She's in her apartment. Tomorrow you'll have your revenge against her, and now we'll go have lunch. Take me through Arlozorov Street, Ephraim. My fault, Ephraim, is that as much as I loved your mother, the purest love of the most loyal man, without a smidgeon of male debauchery to tarnish any thought—I always continued to search for Adela. I'd walk the streets, searching. Your mother thought I needed to walk so I could think about business matters. I didn't even know what I was looking for. And that's how disaster found me.

I wasn't looking for any of those disgusting things men crave, Ephraim. I want you to understand . . . when I was a child and I lived on the second floor, and she lived across the street, on the bottom floor, I would look at her every day through a crack in the balcony shutters. I had to be secretive because people thought they were witches. Satanic witches from the Ukrainian forests. And for better or worse, they never spoke to people, only cleaned their house every day, twice a day, and sometimes they ate colorful fruit, sitting on small chairs on the balcony. I followed her movements. Everything she did was wonderful to me, and I was only eleven. I didn't know if she even realized I existed. But my head was bursting with thoughts of her. She only ever played alone, and swept the floor in swift motions with her grandma, like a big witch and a tiny baby witch. Together they dipped their bare feet in puddles of soapy water, and together they dried themselves in the sun, sitting, eyes closed, on tiny chairs. Everything on the balcony, right in front of me. To this day their hair shines in my memory, as if they were here now and I could just reach out my hand and touch them. I would watch them and think, *Could she be looking at me, too?* But I never really believed it.

And then one time, a knock at the door, at our door, and Mother yelling, "Eliyahu, get the door, I'm not dressed for company."

Adela, the girl, was standing at the doorway and said, "My mother's sick, so I live with Grandma." Then she ran away.

I stood at the doorway like an iron gate blocking a fortress, and Mother called out, "Eliyahu? Is it Uncle Kalman? Is it Uncle Ziggy? Is it Uncle Eliyahu?" I just looked at the empty spot, the one that a moment ago had contained her feet in black patent-leather shoes, like footprints that don't exist but can still be seen. How can I explain it, Ephraim? An angel walked there, and every good part of my soul walked away with her.

Never mind, Ephraim, never mind. Memories, what are they? Nothing. Transparent things inside our heads. Nothing but trouble.

Ephraim, you need lots and lots of energy. Come, let's go to that restaurant you like. Noodles with beef, remember? And soup. And you'll get dessert, too. Come. I hate it when you take me through here. The Labor Federation House, *tfu*—I spit on those ratbag Nazi crazies from the Mapai party on Arlozorov Street. Their time has passed—oh, how it's passed—but from here it looks as if they still rule the Land of Jews. No matter. What's important now is my plan. Our plan. Come, Ephraim, sit here on the bench for a while. I hate talking forward when you're behind me. Come, we'll rest for a bit. I want to see your beautiful eyes, Ephraim, your mother's big, pure eyes, as I explain to you what we're going to do. Revenge, Ephraim.

For her.

Rachel . . .

I waited for so many years, and then a disaster happened and made me a cripple. It was like a test. To see if I'd give up. What can a cripple do? A cripple, alone, against the devil and the devil's family—is that possible? But I'm not one to give up. "To die or conquer the mountain," Ephraim. To die or conquer the mountain.

Let's keep going, Ephraim. Yes. Push me faster. Your restaurant.

You see, for my plan to work, I needed luck. For example, luck to keep that bastard from dying in a car accident. Every morning when I woke up, I worried he might have been run over or had a heart attack. Died, just like that, without knowing he was going to pay for what he'd done. But I got lucky. He got a family of sickly kids, that Dr. Andreas Levin, damn his name. All weak, confused, barely suitable for marriage. And then it happened. A disease of the blood took him. And just like I wanted, he died slowly. I followed him carefully, made sure to come at the right time. They took him, Ephraim, to the hospital, for one final attempt. Only then did I go to see him. *We shall pay you back, Cain.* I remember it, Ephraim, every detail. I came to his bed with a giant bouquet of flowers, the biggest I could find. He was lying there attached to all sorts of tubes, knowing he was never going to get up. I sat down at his side with a big smile and put the bouquet on his body, almost covering him with the flowers. He got angry. Thirty minutes before he died he still had energy. And nerve. "Who are you, sir?"

We shall take the souls of your young.

I explained who I was. Ten years earlier I'd already told him exactly what I was going to do. But he was the same then as he was throughout his life. He threatened me and had the police come to my house. And that was the end of it, or so he thought. You hear me, Ephraim? Watch out here, those pipes again. Who puts pipes in the middle of the sidewalk like that? Goyim.

So I sat down next to him at the hospital, politely, and just reminded him who I was, who you are. Pleasantly, no shouting. I even smiled. I let it be sweet, my black revenge. I showed him a picture of your mother, Ephraim. I pulled it out of my shirt pocket and shoved it in his face. "Rachel Selfter, remember?"

Stop for a second, Ephraim. Just a second . . . just a second.

I'll explain it to you, Ephraim. After your mother died and I was left with you, everything was so black, even the tiniest breath burned, and I started asking about what had happened *there*. To my father, who was murdered there, in the Holocaust. My dear, wonderful father, whom I didn't even know. Mother was smuggled out at the last minute by Bruno Schulz's friends. I've already told you, never mind. And I went to Yad Vashem in Jerusalem one day. With you, Ephraim. Because where was I supposed to leave you? Where could I leave you?

I thought I might find something, someone who might know how the important librarian Ephraim Selfter had disappeared from the Warsaw Library. Your grandfather, my father. I didn't find anything. But there, among all the dead and dead and dead, that's where I realized what my revenge was going to be. That's where I learned that if one man dies, it's no great loss. If his grandchildren are here, he's here, see? The past is here, in the present, and there's only one way a man can really die: if everyone he's spawned dies. His grandchildren, Ephraim, his grandchildren. And that's what I explained to Dr. Levin, damn his name to hell.

Go on, Ephraim. Straight ahead. You have to understand—people love their children, but it's never simple. The ones people love without a shadow of a doubt are their grandchildren. That's what counts. That's a love that's truly boundless. So that's what I decided to take away from him. You see, Ephraim? I sat at his bedside with a picture of your mother in front of his eyes and explained what was going to happen. That I wasn't going to kill him, or his children. His grandchildren, all of them, every last one, and there would be no memory of him in the world. "We shall pay you back, Cain! We shall take the souls of your young." I explained what Jabotinsky had said. Not that I needed to. He was an educated man, damn his name.

I spoke all the names of his grandchildren. Slowly, one by one. Name by name. So that he knew that I knew and had a real plan. I told him, "Get well soon," and left. He yelled, tried to yell, that's how I knew I'd scared him. That was how he was going to leave the world. In a chariot of fear. Oh, Ephraim . . . I'd never been so happy in my life. Maybe once, when I saw your mother, Rachel, up close for the first time. She was dancing at a summer café. Did I ever tell you about that, Ephraim?

CHAPTER 10

ZOE AND RAI

In the end that annoying girl, Zoe Navon, was the key. The break-through. She promised to help and pulled out a thin, tattered white book called *The Street of Crocodiles* and announced that no matter what, she always carried that book in her bag. Like Advil against headaches. Like pepper spray against maniacs. This is a book she carried against the entire world.

She took a nap in Superintendent Jonah Merlin's car, a sound sleep that lasted fifty minutes through traffic from Netanya to Tel Aviv—just like that, a detective and a pretty young girl dreaming next to him—this girl with her tattered book. From time to time, just for a moment, she'd opened her curious eyes, saying nothing before returning confidently to her baby sleep—and after that sleep, from which she awoke just as he pulled into the station's parking lot, without knowing really where he should take his passenger, Miss Zoe Navon kept her promise.

Her hair was wild, a little flat on the side that had rested against the window, and her pretty eyes were completely alert as she pulled the white book from her bag with a smile and flipped through it confidently. She pointed to the sentence written at the murder scene in south Tel Aviv.

Then he tested her on "All books aim at being authentic." He still hadn't told her anything, not about the murder scene in south Tel

Aviv and not about the murder scene where they'd met, at the hotel in Netanya.

She flipped through the pages again with as much confidence and speed. There it was. With her finger, long and thin, a pale ring on its top third, she pointed to a sentence in the book. The sentence from the new crime scene. The same book. The same writer.

Bingo. It connected. But *what* exactly connected?

"This book was written by a man named Bruno Schulz, but don't try to arrest him, Mister Cop, the Nazis killed him seventy years ago."

He gave her his sharpest look—the look of an investigator about to pull out the guts of a difficult suspect.

Where did that confidence come from? An hour of napping?

"Now listen, Zoe. I'm about to tell you a secret. You promise to keep it and tell nobody?"

"Wait a minute, wait a minute. Maybe I don't even want to hear it? Maybe too many people have poured their disgusting secrets into my ears, and since then, what's between my ears is Zoe Navon? Maybe I shouldn't hear your secret?"

"Listen, I'm asking you to help with an investigation. Not a private secret of mine. Nothing personal. A murder investigation, you see."

"Do you pay?"

The nerve. Maybe he should sniff around a little, find out why she isn't in school. Put some pressure on her. Squash her, if he needed to.

"I'm just kidding. I'm willing to help. What?"

He breathed slowly. Watched her, to see where her eyes would run away to.

They didn't.

Like two slow trains, her pretty eyes rode toward him.

"Okay, Zoe, this is just between us. You're practically my first assistant on this investigation, all right?"

"Why don't you raise the age level on this conversation?"

What an annoying girl. But maybe he was annoying her, too. What did he know about teenagers, anyway, or what the world looked like to them?

"The sentences I told you about, that come from your book—"

"From Bruno Schulz's book. A Jewish Polish writer, 1892 to 1942."

"From Bruno Schulz's book. I'm not really supposed to reveal any details from the investigation to anyone, but . . . those sentences were written very carefully at two murder scenes. On the wall right across from the victim. Graffiti. One at the scene from this morning, and the other at the scene of a murder that took place a few days ago in Tel Aviv. Does any of this give you any ideas? Associations? Anything?"

Zoe looked at him carefully. Then she shook her head, slowly, sweetly. She was so pretty.

"I have no idea."

What was the connection between two murder scenes in 2012 and an obscure book by an author murdered seventy years earlier?

No connection.

But Superintendent Jonah Merlin already had an idea.

Graffiti. He had to call that guy again. Rai Zitrin.

"Listen, Zoe, let's make a deal."

She fixes him with eyes that a moment ago were still a little lost and are suddenly sharpened into an all-business expression. Maybe she'll make his life miserable with some hard negotiating. *But why?* He only wants to ask for a little favor.

"I want us to meet someone together. He's a little weird . . . a graffiti expert."

"What's weird about a graffiti expert?"

"Um . . . never mind."

"No, because my dad's a lawyer, and that's a lot weirder. And my mom, you want to guess? A lawyer, too! Have you ever seen what lawyers do?"

"Okay, listen, I want to meet this guy and bring you along as a Bruno Schulz expert—hold on."

He has to answer his phone. Efi Flint from Forensics. Turns out, Captain Flint's people found an unused gun at Julian Levin's murder scene. A strange gun. Very strange. Merlin is invited to come get an impression. Kelsitz is already there and is very impressed.

When he returns to Zoe and their deal, he finds her looking through his CD collection. Hadas's collection, really.

"Play Rage Against the Machine and I'm yours. No matter what you want from me—I'm in."

"Good, Zoe, thank you. Really, thank you. You'll see. It could even be interesting for yo—"

Her look stops him short. *Don't bore me, Officer. I've spoken to more school counselors than you can ever imagine . . .*

"Okay, I'm calling him. And before that, I just have to . . ."

He wants to promise her some candy. Or hot chocolate. To treat her. Rage Against the Machine start singing "Know Your Enemy."

———

The call from Superintendent Jonah Merlin caught Rai Zitrin in Jaffa. He woke up that morning not at home. After carefully brushing his teeth and finding something to eat in a crate that doubled as a fridge, he went out into the street. Rain. What a rainy year. Thunder. Lightning. Giant waves of electrified air. His feet took him to Taboo's rehearsal studio. Taboo was the leader of a young punk-rock group called Mashed Po-titties. Rai assumed he was the biggest ticket buyer for the group's pathetic concerts. They didn't really have any good songs, and punk had already died long before they were born, but he loved watching them as they stood onstage, screaming; loved to look at the audience going wild, and at the pale fans, who knew that their turn to enter the game came after the concert, backstage, and until then did nothing but drink. Rai loved the interaction that hovered in the air, strong and clear. He loved standing there, with a beer, and being present. Taboo never hurt anyone, not even the girls who practically begged him to, and Rai thought he looked fragile and lonely as he stood onstage, hailing every form of evil. "Alone in the forest with a knife and my teacher." "Annoying neighbor and a sack of potassium." "My girl, you're tied up." Taboo screamed the words, and the audience broke them down with alcohol-laden mouths, as the band's mediocre musicians swept everything up into musical dust.

Taboo. It was kind of funny when the name went through the wood chipper of state-issued IDs and became Yochanan Reznick.

Yochanan "Taboo" Reznick's tendency toward dark corners allowed him to discover graffiti in places Rai never would have imagined. The deepest walls. Each time they met, Taboo sent Rai to an address, and Rai went there to find hidden gems. In return, Rai mentioned the band in his column from time to time. "Publicity"—that's what Taboo called it with grave seriousness.

Taboo—twenty years old, fair, skinny, no employment history— lived mostly off compensation from a car accident when he was seventeen. Rai thought he was incredibly smart and had incomparable knowledge on irrelevant topics. His daily wanderings among the shelves of the Beit Ariela Library provided him with endless expertise on any subject. He was also probably the only punk singer in history who sang songs with lyrics by poet Uri Zvi Greenberg.

If the black cat comes to the jug to lap
the remains of the white milk and turns the jug to
   the floor
I will close my eyes and sleep forever more—
never mind, never mind.

He used to sing Ze'ev Jabotinsky's "We shall pay you back, Cain! We shall take the souls of your young" at the end of each show, like an anthem, shattering the words in his mouth before they reached the ears of the drunks, pressed up against the stage, drenched with sweat.

Just as Rai was about to descend the eight steps to the studio, each step crooked in its own way, like Tolstoy's unhappy families, his phone rang. That cop again.

Maybe he had decided to apologize. That joke with the coupons.

Maybe Rai would be paid after all.

———

Rain shook the gutters and in every yard awakened the sounds of tin, loose objects, and free-hanging cables. Inside the café, the servers tended toward dreamy postures. A few of them thought practically about bikes left in yards, plans to be canceled. Others thought of the low sky, the sadness in the air, the things that happened only to them.

Rai and the girl looked at each other.

"Nice to meet you, Zoe Navon."

She gave him a noble hand and smiled with the pleasantness of an event hostess who wouldn't lose her cool even if the Elephant Man appeared before her. At first he thought she was a cop. Maybe a secret agent?

"Don't worry, I'm just a part-time high school student."

It was as if she'd read his mind. He noticed her glancing at his muscles. Everyone always wanted to touch them. But her eyes expressed boredom. Ridicule. Well, he wasn't going to take it personally.

"I'm Rai Zitrin."

"What's 'Rai'?"

"What's 'Zoe'?"

"I was conceived at a zoo. The chimpanzees' cage. Where did your parents do it?"

"Enough." Merlin extended calming hands toward both of them. He was in the middle of a string of phone calls and hadn't even looked at his menu yet. Neither had they. "Or-der," he mouthed at them, but they preferred to eavesdrop on his conversations. DNA, A-positive blood type, textile fiber. Then *Peter Pan*, ticket conversion, expiration date, discounts for Defense Forces. "Did you order?" he asked when he finally hung up.

"We don't make a move without you," said Zoe.

"Okay, I need a giant cup of coffee and a cake with lots of sugar. How about you?"

A waitress came over. Zoe ordered a double omelet sandwich, a green salad, hot chocolate, and a cheesecake. Rai ordered an espresso and a small babka. The waitress wrote it down slowly.

"I have a lot of gay friends," Zoe said.

Merlin turned his head for a fraction of a second. A small surprise, a new view of Rai in light of the information Zoe had presented so crudely. Then he looked away. Not fast enough.

Rai fixed the annoying girl with a withering stare. As much as he could. But his thoughts were bitterly fixated on something else. He'd hoped to gather his courage and ask the cop for compensation for his time, but now he couldn't, because of this girl. He wasn't going to humiliate himself in front of her.

Merlin realized that if he wanted to make any use of them, he had to lead the conversation.

"I want us to start talking about the investigation. About your help. And I want to ask you, Zoe, to show a little respect for all of us."

"I'm not gay," Rai suddenly said.

Merlin and Zoe looked at him.

"I'm not gay."

Merlin's plan was simple. "Undeveloped," in Zoe's opinion.

"I believe the murderer has some experience with graffiti. He didn't start at the murder scene. Murderers like that don't work that way. They prepare. They practice. That's their profile. Now, if we can find a place like that, we might find him less careful there, because he thinks no one would check there. Maybe that's where we'll find his mistake. Maybe. It's a lead. It isn't much, but it's the best I've got for now."

He thought, *I've got DNA from the first scene, but so far nothing's come of it. And who's the victim, anyway? So far no one has reported her missing.*

"I've done a lot of thinking," Rai said. "I went through all the graffiti I can remember. Nothing seems similar."

"Maybe nothing is. But Zoe knows a lot about this writer, whose sentences were already written twice—"

"Bruno Schulz."

"Yes. So maybe she can tell us about him, give us some more famous quotes . . . I don't know. It's kind of a shot in the dark. But maybe that'll remind you of something."

"I love it when everything is so clear," said Zoe.

Their food arrived.

CHAPTER 11

A WALK AROUND TOWN

I ended up taking a walk. A walk with a funny, nice cop, really sweet, and with some kind of journalist. A walk. That's your life, Miss Navon, you never know what kind of comedy you'll be part of on any given day.

What did they want? For me to tell them about Bruno. Like I was a literature teacher. All my trouble in life started because of a literature teacher. If I ever spray any graffiti myself, it would definitely be: "Carmela Tzedek, may the cancer beat you." Because that's what she has. Cancer. She's had it for twenty years. Twenty! People get cancer, heal, die. Even my dog, Tintina, died of cancer. Two months after she stopped eating. But Carmela the teacher has been sick for twenty years. So what? Because of this, she wins every argument, automatically? You're not allowed to upset her. You're not allowed to exhaust her. She started out a young teacher, got sick, and for the past twenty years no one's allowed to do anything to her. Miss Carmela is "coping." She was never willing to see my talents in the classroom. My talents were not in the syllabus. My talents got in the way. Because of my deviation from the material we weren't going to finish covering the material. Wow, we won't finish learning everything and we won't pass the final exam. Someone will come in and see thirty dead students in the classroom, and all the tables upside down, and a goat eating our notebooks. Because we didn't finish covering the material. And in the corner, crying sorrowfully: Miss Carmela Tzedek. Coping.

So I told the cop and that guy, Rai Zitrin, who I felt a little guilty about attacking earlier, that I was no lit teacher, that lit teachers were all old and senile, and then it turned out the cop's wife is a lit teacher. Awkward! Zoe Navon, you're such a Zoe Navon. But how is it my fault? She brought it on herself.

Then that Rai Zitrin, who, it turns out, writes a very popular news-paper column, and we'll see how he can help me out, suggested I just start talking about Bruno Schulz, because we were in a race against time, and just like that, with the authoritative voice of someone who's spent the past twenty minutes sitting in the passenger seat of a police car, he told Merlin, "Maybe we should go to the graffiti place in the meantime? The murder scene? Unless you've cleaned it up . . . Why don't I take a look at it? It would be better than a picture."

That's how our field trip began. Riding to a real murder scene at the edge of town, with me telling them about Bruno Schulz.

"He was born in 1892. Is that helpful? No? Okay, moving on. He was born in a small town named Drohobych in eastern Galicia. Is that a clue? Did anyone hold a gun in one hand and spray 'Galicia' with the other on a wall recently? No? Then, with your permission, I'll carry on. Actually, let's jump to the end. There never was and never will be another writer like Bruno Schulz, and that's something I can't explain to most people, because most people are stupid. Bruno's stories have some sort of protective film around them, so that half the people who see how excited I am about him go read him, and twenty pages later say, 'Damn, what a piece of work, how can you even read this?' Then they go back to the lit final exam material assigned by Carmela Tzedek, and to any book sold two steps into the store. One step, two, and if you don't crash right into the pile of books they want you to buy, written by some woman who cries all over the newspapers about her fertility treatments, game over. Really, it's hard to get into Bruno Schulz's world through that protective film, but those who manage to get in . . ."

"What's his style, more or less?" the cop asks me.

"I don't know. Carmela Tzedek might know."

"Who's Carmela Tzedek?"

"She's *tzedek*, justice. Never mind . . . He writes something like fantasy. But it isn't about dragons and sorcerers, Officer. It's something else; everything's mixed up, the world of a child and his city and his father who loses his mind, and forces of nature all around, and really . . . really, I can't explain it. I'll end up getting a new appreciation for Carmela Tzedek."

"And we'll never know who she is," Rai Zitrin comments.

It's already clear that Officer Merlin and Journalist Rai are teaming up against me. Once again, two against one. Not that I haven't had worse. Even in bed—two against me. Gilly Miller, that son of a bitch.

"Zoe, sweetie, listen. We're trying to find a lead for this case," says Officer Merlin. "We're trying to prevent another murder. Why don't you try and think about it for a few minutes. What about Bruno Schulz's stories or style could have anything to do with murder? Hate, blame, envy, aggression, something . . . anything you can think of. Go for associations, sweetie."

He's called me "sweetie" twice. Death sentence. But no matter, he's sweet himself. If Rai Zitrin called me sweetie, I'd go to his house and tear all his dresses. But Officer Merlin isn't so bad. It's lucky he announces we've arrived, because what I have to hide most of all from Officer Merlin is that I don't even care if there's another murder. Big deal, one less. Wham, bam, another expendable nobody bites the dust.

We go into this building. Let's just say I've seen better.

"This is where it happened," Officer Merlin explains.

Just like a field trip, when Katzman the Bible teacher gets all excited and declares, "This is exactly where it happened!" while we stand on a hill with nothing on it. Then Officer Merlin points his flashlight at the wall, and there it is, Bruno's sentence. I start crying, possibly disrupting an investigation. At first he comes over to me, that nice Merlin. Then, carefully, so that I don't misunderstand, he hugs me a little, and then hugs me completely. I tell him I'm all right, that I'll be all right. Really, his hug is fine. I can feel him making sure not to touch my boobs, not to press me against his crotch. Poor guy.

I stop crying and say we can keep going. Then Rai Zitrin, an A student, as if he'd been waiting this entire time for me to cut out this childish display, starts talking right away. He invites Merlin to look at the lettering with him from about half an inch away, as if he's about to draw all sorts of conclusions. Everything we couldn't figure out yet because I was unable to explain Bruno.

Rai tells Officer Merlin, "Look, when you use a stencil, some people tape it to the wall and then spray, and others don't. Instead, they hold the stencil with one hand, and then, in the middle, they have to switch to holding it on the other side, with the other hand. And then, usually, even with the most careful artists, there's a small visible shift. There are no tape marks here, but also no shift. That's a little strange."

"Any idea how that can happen?"

They both shove their heads close to the graffiti, trying to find a clue. They've forgotten all about Zoe Navon.

"I have no idea," says Rai.

"What if two people hold the stencil?" I ask from behind.

"Two?"

"Two. Then you don't have to switch hands in the middle."

"That's an idea," says Rai.

What a moron. He's been writing about graffiti for like a million years, and this simple notion never occurred to him. On the other hand, if it weren't so dark, I might be able to see the appreciative look he gives me. Because there has to be one.

"So? Should we consider the option of two murderers?" the kind-of-nice Officer Merlin wonders.

That moment a thought cuts through me like a sword: Julian. My Julian. I'd forgotten he'd been murdered just this morning. This morning . . . that's all. Two people walked into our room and . . .

I think I have to call Mom. Have to. Mom, I'm calling you.

CHAPTER 12

The Silent, Wordless Ephraim Dreams a Dream Not Meant for Him: 1914, Bruno Returns from War

"Hello, Bruno, my son, have you returned from the war?"

"Yes. Home."

"And how was the . . . war? Did they hurt you, my son?"

"No, Mother. In fact, there was no war. It never ended up happening."

"But Archduke Ferdinand was murdered, and the nations declared—"

"Yes, Mother. But at the last minute everything was resolved peacefully. You know humans are good. They can make decisions serenely, even on complex issues like revenge and hate. That's what diplomats are for. Creation is good, Mother; it's been proven."

"But Bruno, several villages were burned right here in our area. And everyone has been drafted. And mothers are crying, knowing that their sons and fathers and brothers and neighbors . . . none will return."

"I've come from the battlefield, Mother. I was prepared for the worst, but my worry was as superfluous as a fur coat on a piping hot day. At the very last moment, peace was declared among the nations.

Blue skies reigned over all. At most, you might see a pillar of smoke in the distance."

"But, Bruno, the newspaper headlines, the fire, the blood . . . even here. Awful, terrible stories."

"I swear to you. Look at my uniform. It's clean. There is no war, and there won't be one, either. Ever. The crisis was resolved at the last moment. I witnessed the occasion. A simple soldier, sent to guard the discussions of the diplomats."

"There will be no war?"

"Four representatives of the superpowers convened around a table in a castle in the location where the worst, bloodiest battles were supposed to take place, those that would leave fields full of skeletons and bullet casings for decades after the awful war would be decided. Every diplomat arrived wearing his national costume, and a row of handsome cadets walked behind them in silence, carrying their country's flags, signs, and symbols. Everything was very colorful, and the silence was so deep that you could hear the air creaking in its impressionless, transparent movements. Each representative brought with him a silver pot containing his culture's signature dish. The German representative revealed a beautiful dish of veal sausage cooked in beer. The English representative took the lid off a rustic Yorkshire meat pie. The French representative brought coq au vin with lightly blanched white asparagus. The Russian representative brought a bubbling pot of sturgeon cooked in a cream broth. Everyone sat down with their silver pots and moved them to the person on their left with a loud clang. Each representative took several bites from the dish served to him. Then, with the same confident clang, he passed the dish, already bitten into, to the representative at his left. Once again, the diplomats ate silently for several minutes, and in time passed the dishes to their left once more. By the time each dish returned to the diplomat who brought it, they were all sitting silently, staring at the leftover food in their pots, with slow, discerning looks. They observed the gnawed bones, the ripped meat, the broken skeleton of a fish, the dissected vegetables. Then they looked at each other, nodding with satisfaction, stood up, shook hands in a hullabaloo of linked fingers. Thus peace was declared forever. There is no war, and in fact there never was."

"Bruno, my son, I believe you. I'm so glad. The mothers are happy. Only Mr. Frederik, the grocer, might be sorry—he wanted the Russians to be crushed once and for all. But I'm glad, and calm. I was so scared, Bruno. Will you eat, my son? Won't you eat?"

"No, Mother. I won't ever be able to eat again."

CHAPTER 13

THE SECOND VICTIM, JULIAN LEVIN

Julian was afraid of this country. Sometimes he hated it, sometimes he loved it, but whenever the airplane descended toward Ben Gurion Airport and some fools sitting behind him broke into a few bars of "Hevenu Shalom Aleichem" ("We've Brought Peace upon You"), he felt a big hand strangling him. At least twice a year, and usually more often than that, he'd fly over to his homeland. His father, who was born in Tel Aviv, had left, never to return. He didn't even miss it. But when Julian began hanging around the synagogue not far from their Liège home, learning prayers and taking an interest in a Jewish agenda, his father didn't stop him from becoming chummy with that "group of bearded monkeys." He mocked him, but he didn't stop him. "Do as you please," he said.

Julian remembered his father laughing and saying, "I'm a diamond merchant in Belgium—that's as Jewish as it gets."

At eighteen, Julian surprised his father and went to Israel to join the army. A lone soldier, with no family around. After a full three-year service and a light injury from a stone hurled at his head during the First Intifada, he returned to Belgium to become a diamond merchant like his father. He was more successful than his father had been. He had kind eyes, good hands, and, most of all, he gained people's trust.

Sometimes it made him laugh. People's trust. What, exactly, did they trust about him?

He never cut off his connection to Israel. But from one year to the next, with no clear reason, his trips to Jerusalem and Tel Aviv became more difficult. But he kept returning, overcoming his fear. He tried turning to religion again, even practicing orthodoxy. He tried. But it wasn't what his soul was seeking. He never, not for one moment, was able to believe there was a God, or any purpose to life, or some ideal to strive for. He liked to donate Bibles to decimated communities in Europe and to fund Talmud and Torah lessons for poor children, benefiting all sorts of bums just because they were born Jewish. It was ridiculous, but it amused him and made him happy. People in his regular synagogue in Liège were suspicious of him: What reason could there be for him to still be single at forty-two if not *that* reason, that sin committed by 10 percent of the human race? He thought that was funny, too. His worst sin was women. He liked them single, married, widowed, divorced, young, old. He bought beautiful women for two hours. He broke single women's hearts just as they began beating, because to them Julian always seemed like compensation for years of disappointment. He easily recognized women whose married life had slightly fractured, and used whatever crack he saw there to break it into a chasm. Every man needs a hobby, and his hobby was striking the tender souls of women.

I'm not a bad person, he told himself.

When he visited Israel, his sexual drive came to a halt. Not only his sexual drive. He lost all of his lighthearted self-confidence. Once, he got lost in Bat Yam and for three hours couldn't bring himself to ask for directions. Every year, the Land of Israel petrified him, paralyzed him. He'd lost touch with his sister, who for years had been stranded in some hellhole in the desert. But he kept coming, twice a year at least. This time his fear was different. Somebody had asked him to come.

An Israeli diamond merchant had called him with a business offer that looked profitable, tempting, but there was something suspicious about it. Despite the many details and the attention paid to appropriate words, something about the offer was not right. And indeed, after a more careful review, he found the whole thing amateurish and full of holes. Julian made his inquiries but found no evidence for the existence of a diamond merchant by the name of the man who'd contacted him. A trap, maybe. But why would anyone want to trap him?

The simple, straightforward solution would have been to figure out the man's real intentions and expose him. But instead, Julian boarded the plane for Israel, a genuine fire burning in his chest. He drank a lot on the plane and took some pills and got worried that his body would be unclaimed when the plane touched down in the Holy Land. But the landing went well, and the fools in coach broke into "Hevenu Shalom Aleichem" as usual. When the wheels screeched a little as the plane came to a stop, Julian was covered in a cold sweat. Was he about to be robbed? What would the robbers take, anyway? He had no diamonds on him, and not a lot of money. Would he be killed? Why? Why would he be killed? He had no enemies in Israel; he barely knew anyone here, and he'd committed no sins, no crimes, had no conflicts, no enemies.

Maybe Jocelyn? But what good would it do Jocelyn to kill him, so clumsily, in Israel? She was nothing but a heartbroken Protestant chick from Antwerp who'd been sending him tearful letters and pictures of herself in silk underwear for two weeks. It wasn't Jocelyn. Or Frank, either. It was nobody. He had no enemies.

For the past week, Julian Levin had been preoccupied with this purely philosophical question: What is the reason for a man's murder? What is the principle, or elemental reason, when there is no motive? Why?

And yet, somebody invited him into a trap. What could someone take away from him, other than his life?

He stayed in the airport for three hours before he gathered the courage to leave for the hotel in Netanya. He thought of calling one of his local cousins, whom he hadn't spoken to in years. He remembered copying their numbers from his address book to his first cell phone, and there they'd remained ever since, defined in his cell's memory as "contacts," though he'd had no contact with them since the days of paper and pen. Maybe this time?

He let go of the idea and took a taxi to the hotel. That's it; he's taken the bait. He had given the name of the hotel he always stayed at when he came to Israel on business to a sham Israeli diamond merchant, and from that point on he was subject to the plan of a man apparently wishing him harm.

He checked in, dropped his suitcases in the room, put his toothbrush in the glass. He changed his clothes and went out to wander the streets of Netanya. What would happen next?

He nibbled in the market, then found a dark place masquerading as a luxury tourist restaurant. Then he downed a few glasses of whiskey at a pub on the beach. He expected lots of rain, wet streets. He'd checked the weather forecast every day. But in this country, it only takes one day of sunshine to erase all signs of rain. He preferred rain and lightning and bone-chilling cold. His home turf. His advantage. He was afraid.

In the afternoon he went to watch the sunset at the beach. If it was going to be a sniper, let him shoot him in the back. Let the bullet explode red in front of the burning sun. Let it be theatrical, beautiful. He didn't look back until the sun disappeared and a burdensome darkness took over the city. He left the beach. Nothing had happened, but Julian felt injured. His wound was expanding, bleeding, ripping him apart. If he didn't call for help, this would be the end of him.

He sat down in a relatively quiet corner of a noisy club. The moment he saw the pretty girl, he knew she was the bandage he would apply to his wound, at least until morning.

Zoe. Zoe Navon. That was her name. They moved from pubs to clubs. She was the kind that was truly available to listen. A dumpster kitten. He could tell right away she came from a rich family. Not a real rebel, not a real outlaw, but the kind that explores the margins, looking for trouble, friction, incidents. A good girl, looking for ways to wring some more sensitivity from her soul.

You don't know this yet, Zoe, but it's impossible to pass a lump of iron through a straw.

She listened to him, smiling. The eyes of a squirrel begging for nuts. Pleading to learn. To get smarter. Looking to justify neglected school, grades, achievements. Here she was, learning from life. That's the kind of girl you are, isn't it, Zoe? Poor thing.

So he talked. About anything she wanted to hear. He even talked to her about Cain and Abel. The murder with the unknown motive.

Maybe she, a young girl, would know something. Say something. Solve his riddle. Why would somebody want to trap him?

But she only fixed him with her lovely eyes. A smooth forehead, a charming smile. No matter, the eyes were truly pretty, and that was enough. Around three in the morning he felt drunk enough, tired enough, destroyed enough to go to sleep. He invited Zoe to his room and promised: he had no interest in sex. And he didn't sleep with under-age girls. He was a good man.

In the room, a moment before he dove into a deep sleep, he thought, *Honestly, if she offered to sleep with me, I'd go for it.* Strange, his sex drive was back.

CHAPTER 14

BREAKTHROUGH

Commander Menashe Bried called an urgent staff meeting. He looked ponderously at his subordinates.

"So? We might have a serial killer in central Israel?"

The morning headlines had posed the same question. Most newspapers knew more of the specifics of the investigation than they should have, and cheerfully spread every last squeal of fear. The leaker was sitting at the head of the table, proudly carrying the name Menashe Bried.

The legal counsel for the Israel Police obtained a gag order for most investigation details, but that closed the barn door after the horse had bolted. The details bubbled on the Internet, in the papers, in smart-ass articles, explicitly, implicitly.

"Jonah, what do you have to say?"

Either everything's a dead end, or information pours in from all directions. Suddenly the details crowd like cats begging on a doorstep. Early that morning, a scared man, a licensed private investigator named Dan Rosolio, had come to the police station and told a peculiar story that revolved around the declaration, "I'm innocent."

A woman had hired him. He'd done some work for her in the past, but this time she only asked him to keep an eye on her during a meeting. Some derelict address in south Tel Aviv, at nighttime. She wanted him to watch over the abandoned building to which she'd been invited and intervene if necessary. That was all. And that's what he did. He stood there, watched her enter the building, and then waited for a long time. Just when he started thinking that perhaps he should check on her in there, inside that dark building, something happened. He wasn't quite sure what. He passed out. When he came to, his head was swollen and aching, and the abandoned building was surrounded by the police. He panicked. It wasn't right for him to leave, he knew. He just panicked. And only when he arrived back home—this was the worst part—he discovered that as he'd been lying unconscious in the vicinity of the crime scene, someone had stuffed a gun in his belt. A gun. An honest-to-goodness gun that was honest-to-goodness not his. He had his own 9 mm Beretta, and this gun, well, this gun looked odd. Something different. He had no idea how it got into his belt, who knocked him out, or, generally, what happened. All he knew was that something awful had happened. Yes, he'd read the papers. His client was that same woman who was murdered. And he's innocent. Completely innocent.

The innocent investigator Dan Rosolio gave Superintendent Jonah Merlin the name of the woman who had hired him, Ronit Halevy. And thus, like a swarm of butterflies taking off together, the mystery of the missing person report filed in Herzliya the previous night was solved as well. Ronit Halevy, owner of a fashion boutique serving the richest 1 percent, hadn't shown up to work for the past four weeks. Her partner at the boutique, who'd filed the report, said that "she'd taken off a few times before," but emphasized that this time her disappearance didn't make sense. This time, Ronit Halevy's life was peaking. She was happily engaged to a finance guy from Monaco. She'd found her niche in the world of fashion, and the boutique was thriving. It wasn't like that one time when a guy left her after a five-year relationship. It wasn't like that other time when the business was in crisis, about to shut down. And it definitely wasn't like that one time when Ronit called her partner and told her she'd swallowed a bunch of pills. No, no, and no. This time something about her disappearance just didn't make sense.

The woman was right.

And now she'd been summoned to identify Ronit Halevy's body.

Merlin noticed that the partner—Adela was her name—sounded quite upset as she looked at the body, but the muscles of her face never moved. A tough kind of self-control. The fingers of her right hand mindlessly rubbed the sheet covering the body, as if testing the quality of the fabric. She confirmed Halevy's identity.

Who were you, Ronit Halevy?

The innocent private investigator, Dan Rosolio, provided the forensics lab with the gun someone had stuffed in his belt. He brought it in a shoe box lined with cotton balls. The ballistics man held the gun in his hand in amazement. It was a rare antique gun, in working condition. A gun that was no longer being made, a 7.62 Tokarev, which explained their inability to clearly identify the type of bullets in the body of the formerly anonymous victim, Ronit Halevy.

Patterns and parallels. At Julian Levin's murder scene, investigators found an antique Webley revolver, an unusual model that was attached to a small spear. It was as if someone had found an arms cache from the days of British rule.

An obvious, but so far meaningless, connection. Two people, Julian Levin and Ronit Halevy. Someone murdered them and went to the effort of adorning the scene with passages from the same author. Each murder involved an antique gun.

Details kept bursting forth. It turned out that the two victims were first cousins. Ronit Halevy had recently asked the Israel Police to help her find her brother Keynan, who had disappeared in the United States.

Ronit's report about the disappearance of Keynan Levin and the report of her boutique partner regarding Ronit's disappearance were connected by a simple family tree. There once were two siblings, Sigal and Ari. Sigal had three children: Ronit, the victim from south Tel Aviv; Keynan, the person missing in the United States; and Iris, who'd died of a disease at a young age. Ari Levin moved to Belgium, where his son Julian, the victim from the Netanya hotel, also lived, while his daughter, Gili, had returned to Israel and was living in a remote village in the desert.

"Then maybe she's the murderer," Commander Bried suggested.

"Or maybe she's the next victim," Superintendent Merlin answered.

———

"Did you set up that Gili person with protection?" Hadas asked him.

"Protection plus investigation. Maybe Bried is right and she's involved in this. She came back to Israel a few years ago, and no one knows what she did in Belgium before that. Zero information. In Israel she has a police record. Two files: one for interfering with an officer on duty; the other for attacking a public official. We've got a guy down at the Aravot Station, a friend of mine, Superintendent Dido Partuk. He'll provide her with protection and run an investigation. She's going to hate both."

"What about that other guy, the brother who disappeared?"

"Keynan. Vadim submitted a request for cooperation to the Americans. We'll see what comes of that. The guy was an illegal alien, but they didn't really make an effort to track him down, until now."

———

Hadas was lying on her back in bed, grading her students' exams. A well-aimed lamp poured light over the papers in her hands, turning them almost transparent. Merlin read a few upside-down words: *prodigy*, *bird*, *Satan*. His eyes rested on Hadas. She was naked, and the blanket modestly revealed the tops of her breasts.

Sometimes it helped to tell a literature teacher the main points of his investigations. Sometimes her point of view gave his thoughts a little push.

"It's a subversive reading of police texts," she'd say jokingly, an irony he couldn't understand.

He sat at her side with a bowl of lentil soup, gorging himself.

"I don't know. There's something off about this whole family. It's too filled with tragedy. And the mother, Sigal Levin, can't be tracked down. She supposedly lives in some orthodox community in Safed, no mailing address or anything like that. And to think her father was a gynecologist famous for his campaign to legalize abortions."

Hadas sat up. The sheet slid down, revealing her breasts.

"Did you say Sigal Levin? The model? Dr. Levin's daughter? You've got to talk to my mother."

Jonah looked at his wife's breasts.

"Listen to me now, not to them. Sigal Levin used to be Miss Israel or something like that, the kind of thing where you win a car. She was a famous model thirty years ago. My mother tried to squeeze herself into jeans 'like Sigal Levin wears' after she gave birth to me. I remember Sigal once talked about her famous father, Dr. Andreas Levin, in an interview. A real character assassination. It made a lot of noise at the time. Today that kind of thing is standard."

"Character assassination. Well, that isn't the worse thing happening to this family now."

"*Worst*, not worse."

"Yes, Miss. Right now I'm looking at you, wondering what I'll be getting out of being married to you."

"I'm grading exams, honey. And the pair are coming home from their friend's house in thirty minutes."

"Thirty minutes is plenty of time," Merlin said, reaching out to gently caress his wife's right breast.

"I'm grading exams. Not available. And you have a bowl of scalding soup in your hand. In general, Superintendent Merlin, you aren't available, either. You said you had to get back to the station. Lies must be kept, just like promises."

Merlin smiled. He put down the bowl of soup, took off his shoes, and glanced at Hadas's breasts again. They weren't young breasts anymore. From certain angles, their hanging, emptied-out appearance saddened him, but when she lay on her back and they turned into fair and lovely globes, he felt blood coursing through his body. He loved Hadas's body. He loved her. He loved the thought that she was his wife. What a trick he'd pulled on life, getting this woman as his wife. Thirty minutes. They had time.

"Thirty minutes. We have time."

"You really feel strongly about this?" Hadas said, dropping an exam paper on the thick blanket.

Merlin managed to spot a sentence written in her handwriting: "Insufficient reasoning," beneath which, in urgent blue writing, ". . . and that's what the poet meant."

"Yes."

She reached out to gather him in, saying, "And we'll be listening for the door the whole time, right? The pair are about to come home."

He thought of the ride he'd taken with Zoe and Rai. Maybe there really were two murderers. Maybe. It was a little too much to conclude from a stencil. But he'd texted Captain Flint, asking him to check the hotel room wall for tape marks or a shift in the middle of the text. He thought of the names he'd only recently learned, which were now a part of his life: Bruno Schulz and Carmela Tzedek, along with famous graffiti artists like Banksy. He thought about Zoe Navon. He knew her type, though not exactly. Her anti-everything attitude, her aggression, her distrust of anything that moved. It usually went hand in hand with dropping out of school and getting body piercings. Tattoos, too, obviously. But she had none of that. She was clean of makeup and markings and holes. Just a few rings on her left hand. She didn't go to school regularly, but she wasn't a lost cause quite yet.

"You're not focused."

He propped himself on an elbow.

"Sorry, you're right. The murder investigation. A serial killer, Hadas. A serial killer, and I have no idea."

"Okay, Superintendent Merlin. You got me in the mood, and I'm pulling my weight, and I expect some reciprocity. So forget about murderers for a moment and be here with me, or I'll disqualify you."

"You're right, you're right. Say, do you know an author by the name of Bruno Schulz?"

They didn't make it. Five minutes later, the boys returned from their friend's house, filled with demands. The friend had an electric helicopter, an electric train, an electric pen, and an electric toothbrush. They wanted it all, and most urgently, electric toothbrushes. One red and one yellow.

"You've got tickets to *Peter Pan*," said Merlin.

The brothers looked at each other.

"He fights with a sword," Ido said, clarifying their lack of enthusiasm. "And we're nine years old already."

He was always their spokesperson, their ambassador, while the satanic mastermind behind their pranks was Omri.

They also weren't excited to see their father in his uniform, about to return to the station for some nighttime work. They preferred to avoid an evening spent only with their mother.

"Because then there's lots of rules," Ido once explained to him.

But he had no choice. Something, some vague puzzle, was beginning to come together, and the clock was ticking. He had to go over all the details and hunt down the information that was still hidden among them. He didn't tell Hadas he'd set another late-night meeting with Zoe Navon.

"No problem. One a.m. is nothing for me," Zoe had told him. "That's when I get going. And don't worry, no school tomorrow. They're repainting the place, so they told us not to come."

CHAPTER 15

TESTING BOUNDARIES

So I had to tell those idiots about Bruno Schulz. Great. Actually, that magician-cop Merlin isn't a complete idiot. He could still do something with his life. Just give me a little time with him, and he'd quit the force and perform at kids' birthday parties with bunnies and pigeons and endless scarves. He told me himself there was a chance. At one point, hoping to touch the heart of seventeen-year-old Zoe Navon, he fixed me with sad, lifeless eyes and confessed he wasn't sure if he even wanted to go on with police work . . . that it's nice to solve crimes and crack complex cases, but that police service was much more than that. And I thought, *Here we go, here we go, we're about to get to the part about his wife, his marital issues.*

Jonah Merlin, Jonah Merlin. You have no idea how many men your age caressed my hair in bed afterward, telling me their wife wasn't happy with them, their wife didn't understand them, their wife didn't understand their dreams.

But I'm finished with all that. I tried men out for a while, and now I'm done. They gross me out.

"You're testing boundaries," one of the therapists Mom assigned me said. She didn't realize I was crossing boundaries without even testing them. Who tests boundaries? How does one test boundaries? Bruno

Schulz's father never tested boundaries. They say he went crazy. Did all the things people don't do. A terrible shame. That's what I explained to magician-cop Jonah Merlin, and also to I'm-not-a-journalist journalist Rai Zitrin. That Bruno, who grew up in a respectable home, with a loving mother and father, was suddenly exposed to the world in all its cruelty. With madness came poverty, and with poverty came misery. As if all those had been waiting for him behind a thin curtain, and then the curtain rose and the play began. Little Bruno, here is the play life has prepared especially for you. Applause!

You get it, magician-cop? Bruno loved his father and admired him so much, and then the tower crumbled. You get it?

"And what was your father like, Officer Sir, Superintendent Jonah Merlin? Tell me about your father."

Just like that, before he could start talking about his wife, I asked him. Just like that, without thinking. And why? Who even cares about this guy's father? Just a nice cop . . . But I asked. Once again, my mouth went off before my brain could examine all the details.

Way to go, Zoe.

The only one who answered all of a sudden was one-day-I'll-be-a-real-journalist Rai Zitrin. He talked about his father, taking up twenty minutes, maybe thirty, of the essential lifetime of young Zoe Navon, to tell us about his tepid, timid father, who never dared do anything he wanted, never took a chance or deviated from what was normative and feasible. A careful man who did everything in moderation, moving slowly, testing the waters. Even when he met Rai's mother, it was all as romantic as a handshake.

That's what he said, and then summed up by stating that he's spent his life fleeing the possibility of becoming his father.

At which point I burst, announcing that, with all due respect to participant Rai Zitrin's beautiful sermon, participant Jonah Merlin never had a chance to elaborate on the subject of his own father.

"My father was fine," mumbled participant Jonah Merlin. And he said no more.

I said nothing for a long moment to give him another chance, but nothing. Such a cumbersome silence, and Rai Zitrin standing on the sidelines with see-through tears in his beautiful eyes. With no other choice left, I returned to my job, telling them about Bruno Schulz, how a sensitive boy had to hide his shame, seeing his father breaking down, so miserable that he lost it, screaming, inventing strange sciences, conducting illogical experiments. What was Little Bruno to do? What would Little Zoe Navon have done if Attorney Victor Navon cried with constipation pain over his chamber pot, flailing his hands and tossing his excrement out the window, screaming? Little Zoe would have been kind of happy. But Bruno saw his father as an ancient prophet calling for his God. And what would Zoe Navon do if she had to lock Attorney Victor Navon in two small rooms in the attic? Hmm . . . But Bruno wrote about his father, who became an expert on exotic birds, incubating eggs ordered from all over the world, raising chicks of all breeds, arranging bird weddings, matchmaking and seducing grooms to mate with brides, creating a wondrous world in his attic, which was destroyed when their servant, Adela, appeared at the doorway one day, armed with a broom.

That's what Bruno Schulz wrote about. He watched his miserable father and decided he wasn't miserable, that he was life's great winner, that he was nothing like Rai's father or Merlin's father, that he wasn't some feeble, no-balls bourgeois who didn't have a right to exist, but the only one who had the guts to really live, in spite of the price of such a life.

"My father wasn't a no-balls. He was fine," mumbled magician-cop Merlin.

But I couldn't stop myself anymore, and I kept insulting Superintendent Jonah Merlin's and journalist Rai Zitrin's fathers, both of whom I'd never met, and it didn't help solve the murder at all. The murderer was free to continue.

Let him continue.

CHAPTER 16

EPHRAIM SELFTER—A RICH MERCHANT AND A BOOKCASE

Ephraim, listen to me. My father, a genius librarian in Warsaw, was the first to realize how great Bruno Schulz was. These days everyone tells stories. These days everyone was the first of their kind and everyone knew everything. Ugh. My father traveled to Drohobych, right? Bruno Schulz's town. This was after they found oil there, Ephraim, lots of oil, and the Jews knew just how to make a buck out of what was going on there, that oil craze. Rich Jews quickly began buying all sorts of pretty things so that every moment they could feel how rich they were and how good they and their lineage would have it. You understand, Ephraim? One of these rich men decided to commission a wonderful modern Parisian-style bookcase from the Slovak woodworker Dorhabyk, to set in the living room, before the envious eyes of whoever came over to eat soup and piroshki with beef and cherries, you see? But then he had to fill those shelves with books, and that's why the rich man summoned my father. All the way from Warsaw! You understand? Just like that! He needed books to fill his void of inferiority because he came from a rich place but had no spirituality, no dignity. So my father packed a bag, kissed my mother good-bye, and left. People at the library made faces, but my father hadn't missed a day of work in years, so they didn't have a choice. It was a little hard for my father to leave my mother because it was a day before a holiday, and this is important for my story, but she told him, "Go," because in spite of everything, she knew how important the crazy fee the rich boor had offered him was. And there, in Drohobych, that rich son of a bitch sat my father down and asked him to advise him on which books to get into Dorhabyk's bookcase. You understand? An ignorant simpleton, not a hint of respect for books, invited my father, the expert librarian from Warsaw, because he hoped his money would make some of Father's honor rub off on him. Such is the way of the world, such is the—watch out here, Ephraim, city hall put a barrier here so wheelchairs can't come through. They only think of healthy people. Nazis. Kick it, bend it out of shape, let them suffer. Yes . . . just like that, hard. You are my arms, Ephraim. You are my muscles . . . like that. Yes . . . Oh, how I fed you. I fed you the best of the best, Ephraim, you never went to bed hungry. People thought I wouldn't make it with you, but they didn't offer any help. You are my muscles, my beloved child. No one can say that Eliyahu Selfter didn't give his life for his son. No one.

You remember about tomorrow? We're going. That woman, she's going to suffer, that black soul. We're going to tear her apart, just like Samson tore apart the lion. You'll avenge what they did to your mother. Then we'll almost be able to rest. It's going to take longer this time; revenge is going to take longer, but don't worry. In my plans, Ephraim, there's no room for the tiniest error. And we'll have Shimshon Krieker with us. In the meantime, take me around Arlozorov, over to Bloch Street, and we'll go to your restaurant. Meat and noodles again today. And chocolate cake. Two slices.

Now listen. That rich boor asked my father for book recommendations, and my father recommended this and that. What was he going to do? You can't teach a bear from the forest how to use silverware. But the blessing of my father's visit to the boor in his palace was that it took place during a holiday, and when it came time to go to prayer, the rich man grabbed him by the elbow and took him to the fancy synagogue the rich Jews of Drohobych built for themselves so that he could seat my father at his side, like a Torah scroll. And there, by chance, in the courtyard outside the synagogue my father met the poor young man called Bruno Schulz, who nobody yet knew was a gigantic, mad genius. But my father knew instantly he'd found his soul mate. Just like that. Just like that, my father and Bruno Schulz became friends. And who was the first person Bruno showed his stories to? Who did he really show them to? Not all those lies the descendants of the oil Jews tell today. My father, Ephraim. My father, your grandfather. I named you after him, Ephraim. Stop here, I want you to stop. Come, rest. Only a moment's rest. My father, Ephraim . . . your grandfather . . . may God avenge him . . .

You need to understand that anyone who touched, even for a moment, the life of that magical man Bruno Schulz received the whole blessing, along with the whole curse. A blessed, cursed life. Do you understand that, Ephraim? Don't say you do, because nobody understands it. Not even my father, not even Bruno Schulz himself. For example, the women Schulz was engaged to. There are three women who are said to have been engaged to him. Talented, beautiful women, with bright futures. All three of them were killed in the Holocaust. That's how Bruno's curse touched them. But they also got to hear him speak, tell stories. That was their reward. He blessed their lives, gave them a time in paradise. Poor man.

Now listen, Ephraim. People said my father lost his mind at the end of his life. Who said this? Liars, misers, cheaters, fools, envious men, perverts, louts, savages. That's who. And why did their twisted tongues within their filthy mouths fashion any words about my father? It began with my father and Bruno discovering they were soul mates. Father, to encourage Bruno, after having discovered his writing talent, decided to leave Warsaw, his cultured life, his fancy city, all the comfort he had as an intellectual with a good job, and move to Drohobych. He told my mother it could help with her nerves and make it easier for her to become pregnant. That was something they wanted, my mother and father, but Mother had difficulties. Father convinced her that in the Drohobych air, in its quiet, her body might be able to hold on to pregnancies.

So they moved to Drohobych. Father and Bruno walked the city together, almost holding hands, discussing their higher worlds. Not just oil-oil-oil, goods-goods-goods, respect-respect-respect, like the crooked people of Drohobych.

Me, Ephraim, I'm a simple locksmith. Even when I was doing well and had my big workshop, I was never a man of letters. I could barely read a few lines before I got bored, but I always had true respect for artists, and I secretly fed some hungry poets. Just like my father, I asked them to my table, along with the workers at the workshop. I didn't just toss some food at them, like they were dogs. They ate and drank and came back again and again. All my life I respected people, Ephraim. My mistake was respecting that doctor, curse his name, too. At first.

But I was in the middle of a different story, Ephraim. Bruno was becoming famous, and he took my father's advice and went to Warsaw with his manuscripts, and the rest is history. The name Bruno Schulz was destined for fame. First in Warsaw, then across Poland, and later in every cultured spot in the world. Bruno was asked to visit all sorts of places, to give people the chance to touch his secret, genius soul. But he—a modest, shy man, practically a stutterer, sweet like fresh jam—he couldn't make it more than two days anywhere else, and always returned to Drohobych as fast as he could. He'd always been like that. Even when he was younger and tried to make something of himself, he went to study architecture in Lvov and came right back to Drohobych, a wreck. And when he was accepted to Vienna's Academy of Fine Arts—the same place where the beast Adolf Hitler wasn't accepted—his soul couldn't take it, and he returned to Drohobych a sick man. He was lucky to have his friends, who knew how talented he was, and what a poor fit he was for a mean, rough world like ours. They found him a job as an arts-and-crafts teacher at the local school. The students gave him hell, but they were only students. At the end of the day he could go breathe some fresh air, meet his friends, and be with my father.

They were like twins.

But then came the years of the Nazi war, Ephraim. First the Nazis signed a pact with Stalin, curse his name, and sketched borders and shook hands, promising not to fight each other while Hitler took over Western Europe, occupying a part of Poland, too. They called it the Molotov-Ribbentrop Pact. Curse them, the two goys. The city of Warsaw quickly fell into the hands of the Germans, and my father, who was living in Drohobych, still a free city, with only a few pogroms performed by the Russians as they took over according to the pact, suddenly decided he just had to sneak into bombed, ruined Warsaw and check on the valuable books he'd hidden there. You see, Ephraim? He'd built a small bunker below our cellar. He wasn't thinking reasonably and decided he had to go there and check on the books, his treasures. Mother did everything she could to stop him. She was able to prevent him from going for many days, but Father wouldn't talk about anything else. He only kept saying how he had to, simply had to cross all the lines, all the borders, get to Warsaw, just to take a look and then come back, maybe bring back a few books with him. People said he'd lost his mind. That's what they said, with their mouths rotten from sugar. But Father insisted. Mother fell ill; she knew no good could come of her husband's obsession, smack dab in the middle of a war where millions were killing and being killed. For a while, it seemed that Father had given up. That's how it is, when a man suffers quietly, not making any declarations: everyone thinks he's given up. But Father was simply concealing his intentions, and in the middle of 1941 he decided to act. It was just before Hitler invaded Russia, breaking his evil pact with evil Stalin. The Germans were about to trample over little Drohobych on their way to Moscow and Stalingrad. And my father, living among all those fattened Jews in Drohobych—it was as if he could sense, in his wisdom, what was about to happen: a wall of flames all over the East, a hellfire. He told everyone who asked, "What difference does it make if it's hell here or hell in Warsaw? I'm going." And like that, while Stalin and his generals and the rest of the world couldn't believe what was about to happen on that side of Europe, my father decided that as far as he was concerned, as long as there was a hint of reason in the air, a tiny soap bubble of logic, he would ride it all the way to occupied Warsaw, to our old house, to the cellar, beneath which was another cellar—his secret hiding place for rare books. Before he left, Mother fell to her knees. She even told him she might be pregnant, and that she had a feeling this time it was going to stick. But Father was so used to the miscarriages, and the inner force pulling him to Warsaw was stronger than any outside force. And so, Ephraim, he went on his way. He didn't know he would disappear, never to be heard from again. Who knows? Maybe he never even made it to Warsaw. And who was the last one to say good-bye to him, a moment after Mother stopped crying on his chest? Bruno Schulz. He gave Father an important package, because he believed Father would be able to hide it until the war was over and that if one of them survived, that person would take it out.

And that was that. When Father didn't come back and the war broke out in the East, Bruno took Mother under his wing. This was before the SS Officer Landau hired Bruno to sort through looted treasures and finally brought death onto him. Yes, Felix Landau. You should know, Ephraim, this man, Felix Landau, this murderous, hedonistic monster, was adopted by a Jewish man when he was a boy. That's why he had such a Jewish name, carrying that name among the other SS officers. Just imagine, a Jew-hater, a lousy murderer carrying the name of his adoptive father, Landau the Jew.

Just like that.

Then the Nazis built their awful ghetto in Drohobych, and all the fattened oil Jews could only dream of their oil at night between one damned day and another cursed day. Then came days when my mother and Bruno crowded in one small room, holding each other, crying, never knowing where my father was, trembling in each other's arms.

When it seemed the end was near for Drohobych Jews, Bruno's fans, Polish Christians, managed to find him an escape route, first to Warsaw and then out of the country, to freedom. They built an entire magical tunnel for this man; all he had to do was enter it. But Bruno—like I told you, Ephraim—who had magical dreams about angelic worlds, who wrote in fiery ink about places even God didn't know the way to, he could not leave Drohobych. A poor, submissive man.

You know, Ephraim, maybe those people who built the magical tunnel for him, who did so many wonderful things, were disappointed when the person who stepped out of it wasn't the great artist Bruno Schulz but my mother, a pure-hearted but simple woman. But these people helped her as best they could. They smuggled her, possibly to Hungary, or maybe to the very heart of Germany, and then to Switzerland. She spent some time in Turkey, that much I know, and from there got on a ship to Palestine. And this whole time, I was in her belly. She carried me.

There, Ephraim, there's your restaurant. We'll get you something to keep you strong. Not that I like this place. These aren't waiters like waiters are supposed to be. These are grasshoppers. Weaklings. But we'll go in, and you'll eat, and I'll explain what we're going to do later. Shimshon Krieker will be here soon, and soon we'll be able to rest.

Maybe Mother should have stayed in Warsaw, to look for Father. But what can we know about what should have been in those hard days? She knew she had a baby in her belly, a baby that was holding on, one that would actually be born. That's me, your father, Ephraim.

They killed Bruno Schulz in Drohobych. They shot him in the street, like a dog. This may or may not be a true story. Who knows? His protector, curse him, the Nazi Felix Landau, had an enemy, the Nazi Günther. One completely ordinary day for Felix Landau, he shot a Jewish dentist, who was Günther's protégé. When the two Nazis met in the street and Landau bragged about what he'd done, Günther told him: "You've killed my Jew? Very well. Now I will kill your Jew."

He found Bruno in the street.

CHAPTER 17

THE LANDMAN BROTHERS

It was 1936. More or less. The Jewish Landman brothers had already adjusted nicely to the tough life on the streets of Brooklyn. Barney Landman, the elder of the two, knew how to drown a man in a ditch in thirty seconds without any noise. Levy Landman, twenty-five minutes younger than his brother, knew how to calculate risks and form alliances with the people who called the shots on the streets. Life was filled with opportunities, and most people were too puny to deny them to the Landman brothers.

Barney Landman didn't care what people said about him, least of all Jews who had no balls. But he definitely knew to take care of those who needed to be taken care of. A fist, a pocketknife, a rope. Whatever it took. He was fifteen when Shimi Aronovich, who used to laugh at Barney for not being able to count to ten, or even nine, disappeared for good. For three months, the Jews searched for him, and his family sobbed, but eventually the police closed the file. At seventeen Barney was already working for Hicksey Ganifiglio, quite an accomplishment for a Jewish kid, and he did all right even after Ganifiglio was taken out. Even his brother Levy was impressed. Levy was a bit more sensitive than Barney. People said he had a good heart beneath that mad head of his.

He was a little uncomfortable muscling people his father's age, most of whom he'd known since childhood. Barney didn't care.

The Landman boys grew up, and life was going well for them. They had a piece of any deal made on the street, plus a protection retainer from all the shops in the area. But then the brothers got in the middle of a turf war. Levy realized they had to find a new direction for their business, and fast. Barney didn't care.

Levy's mind worked nonstop, but he wasn't coming up with alternatives. Their name lost some of its clout on the streets. In the meantime, Barney got involved in something completely different. He got himself married to a widow over twenty years his senior. Adela. A crazy, wild, dark-eyed woman with a daughter who never spoke a word. Levy suggested to Barney to put her in the East River. She frightened Levy more than all the tough guys who wanted to kill him. But Barney ignored Levy's concerns. This meaningless marriage changed nothing in his routine. Levy figured they'd have just their fun in the streets for a little while longer, until those threats of revenge caught up with them.

In the barbershop one day, Levy flipped through an article in a Yiddish magazine about the flow of Jewish people to that scorching piece of land, Palestine. His heart suddenly surged with warm feelings for that place over which Jewish dreams floated, and to which Jewish mice fled from all over Europe. He left the barbershop shaved, perfumed, and a Zionist.

He spoke to Barney that night. Their business in Brooklyn was as finished as the back of a traitor's neck, anyway, and what could be better than a place to which terrified businesspeople from Poland and Germany were fleeing? *We'll go to Palestine,* Levy said. *We'll build a territory. What's the worst that could happen?* Barney didn't care.

Thus, at the end of 1936, the two of them disembarked a ship at the port of Haifa. Legal immigrants, with suits and suitcases containing items that were best not to send in the container. A few guns, for instance. Before they left, in order to get together as much cash as possible, they did a few very brash things around Brooklyn, the kind that only sick, suicidal people, or Zionist Jews, would have tried. The Landmans left behind them some Irish and Italian guys who swore revenge.

Levy and Barney Landman went from Haifa to Tel Aviv, where they found their first apartment, not far from Dizengoff Street.

Things went well at first. It was just a matter of reaching out and grabbing a fluttering Jew, newly arrived from Germany or Poland or God knows where, who had some money and was too scared to say anything. Business grew. Arab Jaffa was also a good place, and the brothers learned who to show respect to and shower with gifts. But Palestine was no Brooklyn. Sometimes Barney landed his fist on a nose, and it turned out the Jew had an entire underground behind him—Lehi, Etzel, groups like that—and in the end the British intervened and put Barney in jail for a year.

And then there was Adela. When they left for Palestine, they left her and her strange daughter behind. But Adela tracked down their address and sent them letters, threatening and promising and begging and making ultimatums.

The winds of war were blowing through Europe, and Levy hadn't yet decided if that was a bad thing or a good thing. There was a flow of immigrants from Germany to Palestine. Levy also had a certain respect for Hitler's gang. They were cleaning up their territory. It was simple— the Jews had lost their honor on the streets of Europe and had to leave. But even within the territory of Palestine, Jews had to pay respect and, more importantly, a percentage of their assets to those in control— British leaders, Arab leaders, Jewish leaders, and the Landman brothers.

Barney got out of jail, and a week later he killed a British officer.

Getting in trouble with the Brits was bad enough, but it turned out that the Brit was a secret ally of the Haganah.

The Landman brothers went underground, going by the name "the Artzi brothers." They moved from one place to the next. They stayed in the cities of Petah Tikva, Rishon L'Zion, and in a kibbutz up north. From time to time, Barney returned to his stash of weapons near Dizengoff Street, beneath their house, and took care of his guns and rifles and machine guns. Between visits, he found out he liked guarding the kibbutz against intruders. And if the kibbutz members were willing to accept him as one of theirs, he really didn't mind being a kibbutznik.

One afternoon out in the field, as Barney guarded kibbutz land, his wife Adela and her daughter appeared before him. Adela placed a calming finger on his lips and ordered him to sleep with her silent daughter in the middle of the field. Barney was shocked. And dizzy. He was weak and trembling. He felt himself remembering and forgetting, all at once. Then he passed out. Or maybe not. He couldn't recall. He did remember eventually obeying. He performed the most biblical act of his life.

A few hours later, the kibbutz members found him. He was sick for an entire month. One strong memory had pierced his brain: the moment Adela appeared. He told her he shouldn't sleep with her pretty, silent daughter. Adela was his wife. Adela hushed him. She said something like, "She and I are the same." He couldn't remember exactly. Barney Landman recovered, but he knew his time was near.

One day in 1948, two months before the end of the British Mandate, as he walked down Dizengoff Street in Tel Aviv to check on his weapons stash, a British officer saw him. A few air bullets later, half a platoon was chasing him. Just as he skipped over a wall, the first bullet caught up with him, and he rolled on the ground, and then he started to crawl toward the hiding place, and then the death bullet caught him. Then a dozen more bullets caught up with the lifeless body.

Barney Landman was buried with no next of kin in an unmarked grave, and Levy, under his alias, disappeared forever in the kibbutz movement.

The Landman brothers' assets were abandoned for years, some of them buried in holes, some in the vaults of banks, and the rest in the form of a nice apartment in the heart of Tel Aviv. In 1953, an older woman with seductive good looks arrived in Israel, carrying proof that she was Barney Landman's legal wife. The circumstances of their marriage were vague, but the papers in her hands were real and legal. She inherited Barney's house, found his treasures, got into his vaults, and moved to Tel Aviv with a young girl, her granddaughter. Their names were Adela and Adela.

CHAPTER 18

BRUNO SCHULZ

She arrived at the station in a taxi, and Superintendent Jonah Merlin told himself, "Don't ask where this girl gets the money. Just don't ask." She got out of the taxi, spotted him, walked over as if this were just an unexciting routine for her, 1:00 a.m. at the police station, and followed him through the hallways with regal Elizabethan indifference. Usually those who joined Merlin in the inner wings of the police station glanced curiously in all directions, taking a careful look at the old, cold, leaking building. But not this girl. She sat down heavily in his office, not revealing any of her impressions, bag still slung over shoulder. Merlin wondered if she was disappointed by the poor appearance of the place and was sorry he didn't at least have a print of Van Gogh's *Sunflowers*, or a poster of some kittens—something like that to improve the atmosphere, other than the small photo of Hadas on his desk and pictures of the boys at one month old, one year old, four, five, eight, and on their ninth birthday, hanging like monkeys from the branches of a mango tree.

"I don't like to have lots of pictures and knickknacks—it distracts me," he tried to explain.

She said nothing. Then she lowered her bag from her shoulder, but not before pulling out Bruno Schulz's little white book, as if it were a folder of important investigative materials. Her expression was business-like. He noticed she'd changed three of her rings.

"I haven't been loafing," she announced. "I thought that letting you read the book or looking for key quotes for you would be a waste of time we don't have, so I decided I had to dive into it alone. I've been thinking: Why would a murderer quote Bruno? What's he trying to tell us?"

He nodded for her to go on.

"So I went to see a friend. He helped me with some consciousness-raising substances."

"You're using drugs, Zoe?"

"I use the kindness of the world."

"Drugs?"

"Are you going to handcuff me? That's happened before, but in a friendlier environment. We were just playing. It was fun."

Merlin gave Zoe an enveloping, examining look. She was cold, matter-of-fact. Something determined. Positive. It was best to let the drug thing slide. He wasn't about to save her or change her. He wasn't about to arrest her. But he still asked.

"I just want to know how into drugs you are. Not as a police officer. I'm asking in a paternal way."

She leaned forward, bringing her head close to his, and whispered, "Please, just no paternal stuff. No good. No good in the sad case of Zoe Navon."

He could smell a gentle perfume. She wore just a touch of it, per-haps to conceal a different smell.

Suddenly her face furrowed, as if some storm within her had reached the shore, breaking against the rocks.

"You know, Mister Officer, I was fourteen the first time I slept with a man. He was forty-one. I didn't plan that reverse digit thing. He was old, and he wheezed when he came. I felt nothing. You know how many older men have fucked me? All kind and nice and fatherly, and all very wise men. So please, spare me the paternal stuff tonight."

"I didn't mean to . . ."

"Nobody means to. It just comes out that way. The worst are the ones who *really* don't mean to, the ones who have pangs of conscience later. They didn't mean to . . . it just happened."

"Zoe, that isn't . . ."

She fixed him with a hard expression. He didn't take his eyes off her. He was afraid to respond, to say the wrong thing, to ruin it all. *What is the right word with which to continue a conversation like this?*

"I haven't been with anyone for a year," she said, as if wanting to calm something within him.

They sat quietly.

"Anyone," she repeated.

"Shall we return to Bruno?" Merlin suggested.

"Bruno."

Then, after saying "Bruno," she fell into a long silence again. *Where is your improved consciousness roaming right now, Zoe?* And what was he even doing here, at one thirty in the morning, with this girl? Maybe, maybe it would help. Efi Flint and his forensics team had already issued reports containing many pages, all basically saying the same thing: nothing. His investigators couldn't identify a motive for the murders of Julian Levin or Ronit Halevy. And down in the desert, Superintendent Dido Partuk thought his assignee, Gili, was no more a suspect than a gerbil. Just an odd woman who lived alone and guided travelers on desert tours.

He picked up the book carefully and flipped through it: "I stepped into a winter night bright from the illumination of the sky . . ."

"I'm sorry for the way I came down on you before."

"What? No, you were right. It breaks my heart the way . . ."

"Cool it, Mister Officer. Listen. 'And I shed tears of happiness and helplessness,' it's from his story 'The Age of Genius.' The child Bruno Schulz encounters the spiritual cornucopia, the inspiration whose dam is finally broken. Don't you ever feel like your life is blocked by boredom? Not just the boredom of spending five minutes standing in line at the bank. A general, limitless boredom, like molasses pouring down on us from the sky, clogging our path—the kind of boredom that leaves you with no direction, nothing but eating-fucking-watching TV? You know it? And in this story, the sensitive child sees a big, glowing pillar of fire that finally provides life with the essence it's missing. Does that ring any bells, about the murder?"

Merlin thought. Not about Bruno Schulz, but about life, his career, his general boredom. Is this really what he wanted to do for the rest of his life?

He yearned for an idea, for some inspiration, something that felt like a lead. If not for the sake of the murder case, then at least for the sake of this girl.

"No," he finally had to admit. "What you said rings no bells."

"Nothing at all? Not even something to do with your own life?"

Annoying girl.

"So, look, Merlin. Here's one direction. I was thinking about how Bruno was kind of a loser. A guy who couldn't get a break. Nobody knew what an incredible writer he was. They belittled him. People. His students. He felt detached his whole life. An outsider, a victim. So maybe our murderer is someone like that, who wants to shout about how no one sees his talent. Someone who feels like Bruno Schulz."

"He's unappreciated so he becomes a murderer?"

"He's also a psychopath."

"Interesting thought, Zoe, but in my experience, about eighty percent of Tel Avivians are sitting around, waiting to be discovered. And lots of them are crazy, too."

"Fine, I gave it a shot."

"You gave it a great shot, Zoe. You're wonderful."

"Okay, stop right there. No positive reinforcement. I'm moving on to the next idea."

"Yes, I'm listening."

"You're sounding like a shrink now. One more minute and you'll grow a pipe."

Silence.

"What's going on, Zoe?"

"I have another idea, which has to do with Schulz's father. Many of Schulz's most famous stories are about his father, who in real life slowly lost his mind before his oversensitive kid's eyes. There was another kind of madness in their family. Two children who died as infants before Bruno was born. Depression, that kind of thing."

"How do you know all this?"

"I've read a lot about him. I learned Polish for it."

"What?"

"Polish. I blew off grammar class, conjunctions, adverbs, all that crap, and sat on the grass, a hundred meters away from the teacher, Miss Revital Gindi-Mualem. While she was busy filling out absence forms on me, I learned Polish."

"Can you speak it?"

"Who would I speak it with? Sometimes I get ahold of some Polish tourists and make myself their guide. People can never get rid of me. But I can read it pretty well. Spanish, too. I learned that because of Lorca. I'm very all-or-nothing, Superintendent Jonah Merlin. Anyway, maybe these murders have to do with some sick and painful experience with a father, or a father figure, something like that."

"So that covers about twenty percent of Tel Aviv residents. Thirty, maybe."

"Is there any connection between the victims? Anything at all?"

Merlin looked at his special team member. *Oh well, the media would reveal it tomorrow anyway.*

"Promise not to tell? I'm not actually authorized to tell you anything."

"I never promise anything—it's a principle of mine."

"Okay, here goes: the two victims are cousins. And there are other stories there. Another cousin is missing in America, another died of cancer. There's only one woman, one living cousin, left."

"Is she being protected?"

"Yes."

"Where do these cousins come together? Who's the patriarch? Do you know anything about him?"

"His name was Dr. Andreas Levin. He died seventeen years ago. No criminal history. He was a famous gynecologist, one of the pioneers of fertility treatments."

"Hold on."

"What?"

"I'm getting a text message. One sec."

Her eyes fixed on the phone's screen. Not a late model. She pecked an answer to whoever was texting her at two in the morning.

"It's Rai Zitrin. He's near some wall. He found a sentence and wants to know if it's Bruno."

"And?"

"No. 'Shards of night hanging there / among the weeds, glowing.' It's Haim Nachman Bialik. Our national poet. It's nice that people spray Bialik graffiti."

"So you're proficient in Bialik as well?"

"Don't tell Carmela Tzedek. Anyway, I told Rai to come over."

"What?"

"To come over. Here."

His phone rang.

"And until he gets here, I've got another idea."

Merlin answered the call.

"Get over here, Merlin, get over here. Arlozorov Street. Another murder. Total horror this time. Total horror."

CHAPTER 19

A THIRD MURDER

The old woman lay shattered on the floor, tied to the ceiling fan that had collapsed and was now at her side, one of its blades broken. A hole gaped in the ceiling. There was blood all around. Trails of blood. Sprayed lines like flashes of lightning. Stream-like. Whiplike.

The boundaries of blood seemed to have sketched a circular shape. It was simple—the old woman had been hung from the ceiling fan. The ceiling fan was then turned on, full blast, and the blood spun and flew about in a circular motion, until the fan collapsed with the weight of the small woman.

On the wall, above the television, red letters read: "Thrones wilt when they are not fed with blood." A primitive shotgun, a kind that Merlin had never seen before, rested atop the television set.

Captain Flint and his people hopped around the apartment with light sparrow steps, afraid to spoil the perfection of the scene, yearning not to miss the smallest detail.

Commander Menashe Bried stood with the angered expression of a man unable to figure out why the mystery hadn't been solved and the murderer captured while he himself enjoyed the sleep of a decent citizen.

Superintendent Eli Levy showed up as well. He could have napped like a sated cat atop his stack of solved cases, but he came to the apartment to support Merlin. Unlike Merlin, he had developed political instincts and an impressive ability to handle himself against the wolves of the station hallways. He knew that hellfire and brimstone would be aimed at his friend. The chief of police had already called. So had the minister of the interior. The prime minister had been notified. Merlin was walking around, looking for guilt, never realizing that one guilty party had already been announced: himself. Levy felt the need to show up and track down the threats circling his oblivious friend. He'd even taken Limor's tears in stride as she protested, "I'm about to give birth! What if my water breaks? What if my water breaks?"

He watched the streams of blood, the hypnotizing circle, reminiscent of the mandalas Limor drew to calm her nerves.

He looked at Merlin, standing focused on the side, speaking to no one.

He looked at the two members of Jonah's small team, Tal and Kelsitz. Both of them felt an obligation to come and had followed their hearts. It was as if they'd all been summoned to the funeral of Superintendent Jonah Merlin.

Indifferent to sealed fates, to the sword hanging over the superintendent in charge of the investigation, two men from Captain Flint's team now crouched by the door. There were four locks on the steel door. The break-in looked professional. The two men carefully examined the broken locks, hoping for some evidence to pop up. Above them, a small sign revealed the victim's name, Tamara Zelipowich. A small stack of mail addressed to her was in the apartment. Was she a member of the Levin family as well? Several officers were already working on finding that out.

Merlin walked carefully to the balcony. There were police cruisers outside, strewn about in no particular order, their red lights circulating. In the darkness and the rain, the lights looked like weighty cherries. Merlin tried to think. The new scene drowned him with details. But it was the same pattern. Nothing new. He had to take in every detail, not let himself get sidetracked.

Kelsitz approached him and said, "Help you, Boss?"

Kelsitz wasn't the kind of man who could sense when a person wanted to be alone, to focus. But Merlin was glad for the distraction. It was good to share his confused preliminary thoughts with someone.

"The first thing I see, Vadim, is that someone put on a show here. This is different than the other crime scenes. That idea of hanging her from the ceiling fan—hate, maybe?"

"A personal vendetta."

"Yes . . . and besides this drama, what I immediately see is a balcony. We walked around the house. All the windows are shuttered. It smells stuffy, no air, the kind of people who never crack open a window, not in summer and certainly not in winter. Only the balcony shutters are wide open."

"Did the killer do that?" Kelsitz wondered.

"That probably isn't something a killer would want to do. Unless it was imperative that he open these shutters."

"To bring something up? To get something down?"

"To look somewhere?"

Kelsitz looked around him, bored.

"Look where? Down at the street? At the house across the way? Where?"

"I don't know, Vadim. Listen, go across the street, check with the neighbors, witnesses. There were shots; there was a murder. Maybe someone saw something, heard something."

Kelsitz was pleased with his assignment. Maybe some civilian would object to the visit from the law. Reasonable force. A little action outside of the office.

Merlin had a few moments to himself. To think. To rack his brain. To think. To focus. Before the reports came in to confuse him with too many facts.

The first murder: amazing force, a one-handed strangulation, marks of attempted cover-up, wheelchair tracks, a quotation from a Bruno Schulz book, a weapon from the days of British rule. The second murder: Netanya, a hotel, no suspects on staff or among hotel guests, security cameras with no footage of any suspects, more from Bruno Schulz, another weapon from the days of the Brits, no motive. No motive. Cousins. Still no motive. Possibly more than one murderer.

Zoe talked about vengeance. About people feeling disregarded. She asked about a patriarch.

Lightning hit somewhere near. In a moment, the drizzle would become rain. Thunder rolled, and a thought hit Merlin. He recalled a different rainy night, that car crash on the way to that village in the Sharon region. His car was stuck and he'd walked over to the police barrier . . . and there was that story about the wounded driver who kept screaming. There was a guy in a wheelchair and a giant. And a third man. He had to speak to the driver. Was the guy still alive?

The image was alive in his mind. Two murderers. A man in a wheelchair and a giant, leading him.

He called the hotel in Netanya, identified himself to the receptionist and told him to find out who was on duty the night of the murder.

"I was on duty," the receptionist replied importantly.

The receptionist wouldn't give any information over the phone. Besides, he knew that the man in charge of investigation was Superintendent Boris Karni of the Netanya precinct, and not Jonah Merlin of the Tel Aviv precinct.

Merlin tried to explain.

Suddenly a hand grabbed his phone. Kelsitz.

"I'm still here, Boss. Give me a moment with him."

He carried Jonah's phone back and forth across the balcony, speaking to the uncooperative receptionist. A moment later, he returned the phone to his commander.

"He'd be glad to help now."

"Thanks," Merlin mumbled.

His question was simple: Around the time of the murder, did an older man, in a wheelchair, stay at the hotel, or even visit it, along with a giant?

"Yes, they were here. How could I forget them? An older man in a wheelchair, and a huge man who pushed the wheelchair everywhere, younger, probably mentally challenged. One moment, this computer is so slow . . . Okay, here we are. They checked in two days before Julian Levin. They left a day after the murder."

"Who booked the room?"

On the other side of the line, Merlin heard fast typing. What had Kelsitz said to the guy? That he was going to come see him privately?

"A company called ASG Management," the receptionist said.

"Who are they?"

"I have no idea," the receptionist said apologetically. "I can check their record. One moment . . . no, they never booked a room here before that time. Sorry. Truly, I'm sorry."

"Thank you."

Merlin turned to face the scene of the crime, the vision of horror. Now he was prepared for new details to arrive.

Two of them. A man in a wheelchair and a giant that pushed him. And another man. A third.

Merlin called over Kelsitz and Tal. He shared his thoughts with them and asked them to dig up all they could about ASG Management. He also asked them to find that screaming driver. He ordered Kelsitz to only go over there with Tal. In his mind's eye he could see the driver, held upside down outside the window as Kelsitz tried to get a few more details out of him.

"Now both of you go. Let me be alone here."

His two officers took off. Tal was gloomy. Kelsitz's face, on the other hand, stretched into a tiny feline smile. Perhaps he was also envisioning the screaming driver hanging upside down out the window.

Merlin left the apartment at dawn. Reporters were waiting for him downstairs. So was Zoe Navon.

He'd thought that after Commander Bried regally descended the stairs to meet the reporters who had been waiting for hours in the rain only to hear Bried perform one of his famous "no comment" pieces, they would all disappear to their cubicles, their computers, their coffeemakers, from which to spread toothy waves of alarm and anticipation of more fear, more anxiety, more terror. And yet they'd been waiting—a raging, determined ring.

On the outskirts of the tumult, leaning on a column, detached and bored, was Zoe, wearing a red rain jacket, reading her white book. She glanced at him and returned to the book.

"Why are the police not revealing the extent of this case to the public?"

"How convinced are you that this is the work of the same murderer?"

He breathed slowly, feeling nauseated, dreaming of coffee. All around him it was as if morning had slapped the birds awake in the treetops, releasing choruses of chirping.

"What do you have to say to the public? Is the murderer going to strike again?"

"What can you tell us at this point? Would it be fair to say the police have no leads?"

Merlin wanted to pull Zoe into his police car, take her home, let her sleep like a seventeen-year-old, on fragrant sheets, surrounded by pink pillows and teddy bears. He walked glumly through the crowd of reporters to his car. From the corner of his eye he saw Zoe walking toward him. "What are you doing here?"

"I was waiting for you."

"But what—"

"Why don't we get out of here?"

He looked back and saw the ring of journalists watching them.

"When will the gag order be removed? What purpose is it serving?"

"Zoe, honey, you should go home and go to sleep."

"Drop it, sleeping hasn't been my thing for a while now. I can only fall asleep next to you, remember? How long ago was that? And please stop calling me 'honey.' I'm no honey."

"What's the next step in the investigation? Is there any truth to the rumor that the police already know the common denominator linking the victims?"

To Merlin's delight, the rain began pouring wildly again, and he grabbed Zoe's elbow and pulled her into his car.

"Is this girl connected to this most recent crime? What is your name, young lady?"

He called his team and demanded to know if any details had been found regarding ASG Management. He gave out descriptions of the potential perpetrators. He called Efi Flint. He called Superintendent Dido Partuk down south, to check if he'd found anything, and if Gili Levin was still alive, and if she'd confessed to anything. He called Kelsitz again and demanded that he and Tal find out where, if anywhere, the wounded man from the car crash was hospitalized, the one who saw a man in a wheelchair, along with a giant and a third person. He called Hadas. This was supposed to be his morning, his turn to take the twins to school, but he had no choice, and she would have to call up the substitute teacher to cover first period, as usual. The poor fellow. The board of education some-how found this East European immigrant who stood before classrooms, pathetic and hunched and trying with all his might to win over his audience, without a chance in the world. Instead, the students' hearts grew harder and colder at the sight of him, at his not understanding the codes for dealing with high school wolves. Merlin spoke to Hadas, apologized and explained, most of his contrition directed at the anonymous teacher, who would have to face his torturers in less than an hour.

"Aren't you tired?" Hadas asked him.

Next to him, deep within her private world, was the sleeping Zoe Navon.

"Just miserable. But we may be getting closer."

"They talked about it on the radio. Everybody's talking about it."

Efi Flint was calling on the other line. Merlin was glad to discover he could now identify "call waiting" on his new phone.

"I have to go, love. Send my apologies to Andrei."

"His name isn't Andrei. Bye, kisses."

He spoke to Efi Flint. The weapons expert had identified the machine gun on the television set at Tamara Zelipowich's apartment as a rare collector's item. A highly efficient 9 millimeter submachine gun, handmade by Haganah hero Joseph Carmi, which had never been put to regular use. Only twenty-five such guns were made, and one of them was placed tonight on top of Tamara Zelipowich's television set.

"Someone really did find a weapons bunker, huh?" Merlin said.

"I hope for your sake that it's a small one. For our sake."

"Yes."

Beyond the windshield, Jonah Merlin spotted a familiar-looking café. *Oh, of course.* He had coupons for this place. On this rainy morning, the café's facade gleamed, fresh and seductive.

"I'm no honey," Zoe said when he gently woke her up.

CHAPTER 20

ELIYAHU SELFTER SEARCHES FOR ADELA

You see, Ephraim? Every mold requires the breaking of the mold in order to survive. Let's say, for instance, that you've got a military code and you want to ruin the chances of anyone cracking it. Simple—just scatter some mistakes in there. Whoever has the key to the code would understand it with a mistake here and there, but those trying to crack it would get lost. Understand? That's why doing this thing that has such a clear mold—it was only a matter of time before they caught on to us. We had to scatter some mistakes. You see, Ephraim? We needed some time. Just a little more time, before we perform our final revenge.

And who deserved to be put on our list more than this lady? Tamara Zelipowich earned her place on the list, and now she's paid the price. It wouldn't have taken much for her to live her small, insignificant life until she died of old age. But things happen, Ephraim. People meet, and things happen. Just like that.

One day we went to the police, you and I, to file a complaint. Miss Zelipowich was standing right next to us, also filing a complaint. I didn't mean to eavesdrop, but she shouted and shouted and I couldn't help it. I heard what she told the investigator, and my heart started pounding. Before my mind could understand it, my heart already realized I might have found my Adela.

Yes, just like that, I admit it. I'd searched for Adela for many years, from the day I came home on leave from the army to find her gone. To find her apartment, her grandmother's apartment, the Landman brothers' apartment, empty. I didn't fool myself for a moment that she'd gone on vacation, that she'd return to me. When I looked from our balcony down to her apartment, I felt the black void of emptiness. "The witch is gone," Mother told me, hugging me from behind like a mother would her son. But I felt I was about to burst with insanity and rage. After all I'd done . . . where had she gone?

I started looking for her, with my mind and my feet. I walked the streets, looking at balconies, completely certain that when my eyes spotted the right balcony I'd know immediately.

But I was a soldier. A paratrooper. I've told you this before, haven't I, Ephraim? I could only look for Adela when I was on leave. Maybe that's why she disappeared on me like that. Completely. Did I tell you about my years in the army? I had a wonderful service, but then during a time of grief I quit and went to work in a remote village. After fighting in the Six-Day War, I returned to the army, to the Jordan Valley. But eventually my hands were drawn toward the mechanical. There was a locksmith in the village, and he taught me everything I needed to know, and I discovered my own calling.

But most importantly, Ephraim, I looked for Adela that entire time. In Tel Aviv, in Herzliya, in Netanya. Anywhere I got the sense she might be. I just wanted to see her one last time.

Maybe she had run away from me?

You have to understand—I knew I'd scared her. She lived alone, a young girl. Where her grandmother, the old Adela, went, I don't know. After I joined the army, I couldn't follow everything that happened in their apartment from behind our balcony shutters anymore. One day, when I came home on leave, I noticed she wasn't alone. There was a man in her apartment. A man. Not only did I have my army rifle across my chest, but also Barney Landman's entire arsenal was hidden in my secret closet. I wanted that man to get out. You understand me, Ephraim? I was so used to Adela not being like the rest of them, perfectly clean, not interested in what girls . . . never. Clean. But suddenly that devil was in her home, in the dark.

I couldn't sleep that night. I snuck into the yard separating our building from hers, and just as I'd done in the Jordan Valley, I walked like a shadow. When I was close to her balcony, when I could already imagine her breath and his breath together in the same room, when I was about to do what was natural for a man to do, because I'd brought two of Barney Landman's guns with me, suddenly a voice sank from the tree above me, taking all the air out of my lungs. I looked up, and a big black owl gazed down at me with eyes as large as moons. The sound it made poured lead into my body. I'd never seen anything like it, certainly not on that half-dead tree in our yard. I barely made it back home. Barely.

I began following her. I'd come home on leave and follow Adela, and I might have frightened her, because once when I came home I saw him over there. The man. A black shadow and a red dot. He must have been smoking a cigarette, the devil. And right in front of my eyes, Adela joined him in the dark, standing right where there was a big square of light in the afternoon. You hear me, Ephraim? Because of the sun, her balcony would have a wide square of light streaming through the window, from the southeast, and when Adela walked through it, or stood within it, it was as if a master artist had created an imperial stamp of golden clay. Just like that. Golden lines. Have you heard of Cleopatra, Ephraim? Think of something beautiful and still that suddenly moves away from the sun square and returns to its own colors, red dress, green eyes, black bow in her hair. And that broom of hers. To this day, when I see one like it at a store on Allenby Street, to this day my heart wants to burst with happiness and pain.

And he was there, and she was next to him. It hurt so badly, Ephraim. It hurt so badly. That's jealousy, Ephraim.

Keep going, Ephraim. Just a little rain. Getting wet won't kill us. Come on, we're not like the rest of these people, made of dust, afraid of getting wet. Weaklings. Go on, Ephraim, take me and listen to my story.

I waited in the street. When he walked out, I followed him, Barney Landman's Lee-Enfield rifle slung over my shoulder. What can I tell you, Ephraim? The entire world was suddenly sucked twenty years back, and I was a boy, and the British ruled us, and Turkish guards roamed the streets. Someone peeked out at me from a grocery store, but I wasn't deterred; I kept going, as if the whole world obeyed my orders. He had a large backpack, the devil, and he also walked carefully, even glancing back from time to time. But I was a veteran soldier. I just kept tracking him, waiting for my chance to present itself. Then, at a street corner, next to the textile store that had been there ever since I was a child, I took the Lee-Enfield off my shoulder and called out, "Hey!" And he started to run like a cat, into a yard, jumping over a wall, and when he was in the air—like that, in midair—I shot twice. Bang. Bang. Silence. The second bullet split his backpack, and as the devil fell into the yard, the open backpack fell on the sidewalk, spilling cigarette packs—red, blue, gold. I turned around quietly, without a care, as if I were the only one to determine when I would leave this universe of the past. Indeed, I walked freely all the way to our building, not like Barney Landman, who'd crawled into our yard, painted red with his own blood.

You know, Ephraim, when I saw him falling . . . I'd never been happier than I was at that moment. That, Ephraim, is a hard thing to explain.

Then I returned quietly to the army. And Adela disappeared.

The papers said a black-market cigarette seller had been murdered. I murdered the devil, Ephraim, but Adela was gone. That was the problem. I haven't had a day of rest since. Not a single day.

And then, Ephraim, at the police station, when I heard that evil hag, Tamara Zelipowich, I realized I'd found Adela. Just like that. The heart knows. I followed her. I knocked on her door and was crafty. She had small eyes, like a rat's. But I only walked into her apartment for a moment, and from the side, through the balcony, I saw Adela's apartment across the street. I'd found her, Ephraim. I'd found her.

You know what snakes in the heart feel like, knotting one another and choking each other? Snakes in the heart are . . . good. After that I had to make a plan, because that woman wouldn't let me stay in her apartment more than twenty seconds. By the time I reached the house I already had a plan. I was going to buy that evil woman's apartment. I would have Adela's balcony across from mine.

At first she said no. An emphatic, vicious no. But when I started mentioning numbers, greed rose in her heart. We negotiated. I had to haggle with her like you haggle with a criminal. I'd planned it all out. And she, that vixen, she was so eaten up with hate, with envy, with . . . it wasn't easy. But eventually we got it done. Our lawyers met. We had a contract. We held a meeting at her lawyer's office, and suddenly . . . you see, I felt that I was committing my important act. That this was a reward for everything I'd been through. I'd given up a lot. Almost everything. And then she said no.

Are you listening to me, Ephraim? Even her lawyer, who was used to all her craziness and her conflicts with neighbors and her police complaints for things that only happened inside her mean little head, even he couldn't figure out what she wanted, why she suddenly said no. And what did she have to say about it? That it was her right and that she owed me no explanations. "No."

You understand, Ephraim?

But I was strong. I had to be strong as a child because things weren't easy. You can't even begin to imagine how difficult it was, Ephraim. And later, too. Even in the army. No one understood me. And then you, Ephraim. That damn Dr. Levin killed your mother, and made you damaged, my sweet child. This damage. And I wanted the apartment so badly. So badly, Ephraim, you see?

So I made a mistake.

I went to her apartment, to that black widow. And I don't remember. I just don't remember. But after I left, I decided I had to look into Adela's balcony, to see her there. It was a nice evening, Ephraim. It smelled balmy, like it used to smell in the fields when I was a boy.

Breaking open the door to the roof of that building was a piece of cake. I leaned on the railing and looked into Adela's balcony. Adela was a woman by that point, just as I was a man. I don't remember what I saw. I'm not sure. But suddenly, the world shook. Within the darkness, I felt something moving, like an avalanche, a mountain collapsing. It was only the railing that broke, but what difference does that make. I fell.

It might have been better had I been killed. But I survived. I fell down one floor, then hung onto something, then two more floors, and only then crashed onto the street.

People surrounded me on the street. They called an ambulance. And I only thought about you, alone at home, about to wake up. Without your daddy there. I was willing to do anything, just not to let you wake up alone.

I wouldn't allow that.

Then I saw a man approaching. I looked at him. I didn't know him. It was Shimshon Krieker, but I didn't know him yet. Still, I gave him the key to our apartment and sent him to you. And then . . . and then I can't remember anything that happened for a very long time after that.

When Adela disappeared on me, I was still young and single and could do things. I didn't just sit around, not living, regretting the years. I opened a locksmith shop: Selfter Locks. At my peak, I employed thirty workers. I was considered an expert. Selfter. From the very beginning, even when I was young and had a small new workshop, people respected me. They made offers, too. Wanted to introduce me to girls, to find me a match. But I was searching for Adela. Then, one day, I saw new tenants in her old, empty apartment. I'd moved Barney Landman's arsenal, all those weapons, to a hiding place of my own, long before that, so I wasn't worried. I was just sorry to think that simple people would fill the space that used to be golden light. Two years later, other tenants moved in. And then your mother's family came, Ephraim. She looked at me from the balcony the day she arrived. She was already thirty years old, almost my age. I was still looking for Adela, and even after we began seeing each other and decided to get married, I couldn't stop thinking about Adela. Her strong hands, playing with the broom and the mop, the duster, how she blew the dust off the walls to tremble like flies in the light. Wonderful. Wonderful. Are you listening, Ephraim?

Even after I married your mother, and loved her, I wanted to find Adela. It was all right. I didn't want to meet Adela the way a man meets a woman. I wanted . . . I wanted just to see her. And there, in that apartment that first belonged to Barney Landman and then to Adela, that's where she lived, your mother. She didn't say much. She was a quiet woman who made clothes. She was tall. That's where you got your height from, maybe. And modest. You couldn't ruin her with bedroom talk. She did what a woman was expected to do—she was fine—but nothing rotten. A shy girl. Only what she had to.

We wanted a child and it was difficult, Ephraim. And then we met that Satan son of Satan son of Satan son of Satan. Dr. Andreas Levin.

Mother was pregnant with you, and everything was normal. We were just afraid. So we went to see him. We thought an angel had opened the door, with his pristine white coat. The way he spoke, saying, "Don't worry, ma'am; don't worry, Mister Eliyahu. With my help, you'll have a child."

CHAPTER 21

THE WISDOM OF THE MASSES

"Are you tired?" She stirred her hot cocoa, looking at his giant cup of coffee with loathing.

"I'm used to it."

"This is your chance to tell me everything about the investigation. You're tired, you don't have any self-control. You won't even remember telling me later."

He thought she was going to say something else. He wanted her to say something completely different.

She sipped her cocoa and said, "I'm hungry. Hey, there's Rai. I texted him and he came."

"When did you do that?" he asked, surprised. "When did you even have a chance?"

What he should have asked was "Why?" But he was just too amazed: Had she been texting in her sleep? Or maybe when he went to see the shift manager about the validity of his breakfast coupons? When? He was floored by young people's command of technology. He'd been left behind, utterly prehistoric. There was that class, Squeezing the Juice from the Internet, that was offered in the most recent *Defense Forces Special Winter Offers* booklet. Maybe he should take it. Maybe he had to.

"What's up?" Rai asked.

For some reason, he was also wearing a red raincoat. *A fashion trend?* He took off the coat with the waterfall sound of nylon against nylon.

A stout young waitress came to their table and set down plates and arranged small dishes with their breakfast spreads—he'd ordered breakfast for two and now would have to pay for Rai out of pocket. He looked at the waitress. The charming contour of her thighs showed from beneath her woolen stockings. *Why is she not in school?*

"I hear there's been a third murder," Rai said, sitting down heavily, looking at Merlin's coffee cup and at the plates of food pleadingly.

"We'd like another breakfast," Merlin told the waitress. "Rai, choose what kind of eggs you want, and which beverage."

"I'll have exactly what he ordered, thanks," said Rai, and Merlin was suddenly very, very tired.

"Yes, a third murder," said Zoe. "And another Bruno quote on the wall. 'Thrones wilt when they are not fed with blood.' It's from his story 'Spring.' And another old weapon on the scene. This time they really tortured the victim. Then stabbed her and shot her. And they did it all in the evening, most likely."

"What . . . how . . . how do you know all this?" Merlin asked, shocked.

"Profound listening."

"What are you talking about? I never told you anything."

"You told me a little. And the other cops. Your hotshot commander spoke to one of the journalists on the side. Is it my fault that it was my side?"

Rai's eggs arrived. Sunny-side up.

"Say, Rai, do you know anything about weapons bunkers? The ones that were left from a while ago? Sometimes they still turn up."

"That's not my area of expertise. Tel Aviv weapons bunkers are the exclusive domain of Abner Party. And no jokes about his name, he's got a hot temper. He's all about weapons bunkers, wine cellars, hidden spaces. Not only underground, but also behind walls and up in attics. He claims to have found a sadist's torture dungeon from the 1930s, but that's a well-kept secret that will come out when the time is right. Probably in book form."

"All right. I might want to talk to this bunker expert."

"Now?"

"Now we eat."

"Just like I said, there must be at least two killers. A guy in a wheelchair and a giant rolling him around," said Zoe, watching Merlin with a pair of pristine eyes. "What? You told someone on the phone when we were in the car."

"You were asleep."

"Among other things."

"Hang on a minute, I know those guys," said Rai.

"What?"

"There's a pair that matches your description. Tel Aviv weirdos aren't my area, but when you walk the streets all day long you can't miss these two. They walk around together all the time. Just like you said, a fairly old man with a blanket over his lap and a giant who looks a little slow, pushing his chair. The old man talks and the giant almost never answers."

"Where do they live? Where can I find them? What can you give me?"

"Let me put out the word to my friends. Probably half of them don't have cell phones, but I'll spread it, and it will make the rounds. I promise you full details by this afternoon. Anything the street knows, you'll know."

"Oh God, make it quick, whatever you can get me. We might be preventing another murder, Rai."

"Done," said Rai.

Merlin realized that the text had been completed in the mere seconds Rai had been holding his phone. Squeezing the Juice from the

Internet. He had to take that class. And maybe also, Your Smartphone Is No Smarter than You.

"Can we go to Jaffa?" asked Rai. "I have an idea for a shortcut. There's someone who knows the streets better than I do."

———

Kelsitz called. They'd located ASG Management and had already talked to the owner, a guy named Shimshon Krieker, who operated the small company that booked hotel rooms, holidays, and flights for people. He was fine, cooperative; he had all the names. He apologized, said his accountant had his documents, and said it would take him twenty-four hours to get back to them with the name of whoever booked the hotel room in Netanya. He figured out by himself that it was important, and that it had to do with the murders.

"I can speed things up," Kelsitz offered, "but I think this Krieker is actually cooperating. I have a good instinct for when people are telling the truth."

———

They descended the crooked steps of the Mashed Po-titties rehearsal studio.

On their way to Jaffa, Merlin had received a text message from Eli Levy: "Don't take it personally, but they're starting a parallel investigation team, and they'll ask you for all your materials. Bried had no choice."

Why should he care? As far as he was concerned . . . Maybe they really did need a team that wasn't trying to crack the case by walking down crooked stairs to a rust-eaten door, behind which they could hear the sounds of a bombing.

Rai opened the door.

"And carpets made of babies! And carpets made of babies! And carpets made of babies!"

As the door opened, someone was actually singing these words, while all around sharp notes and mighty gusts of bass exploded into the room.

"He means metaphorically," Rai shouted.

"So he's actually talking about the occupation of Palestinian territories?" Zoe shouted back.

Rai didn't answer. He led Merlin and Zoe to another door, where it turned out they had yet to experience the music in its full intensity: when Rai opened that door, the sounds burst out, shattered tails of voices, and Merlin's ears began throbbing. Then, all at once, the music stopped.

When their eyes adjusted to the dark, they could see the three musicians, who were looking at them tensely, especially at Merlin in his police uniform.

The lead singer collapsed in a chair, his chin against his chest, curling into himself. Rai quietly signaled for Merlin to wait. They had to wait a few minutes after his singing and before addressing him, the way you wait a second before opening the door of a washing machine that has just finished.

Merlin spent this respite scanning the rehearsal space. Art reproductions all over the walls. Parmigianino's *Madonna with the Long Neck*. A repulsive photo of something that looked like a goat's guts spread over a table. A black-and-white photo of a pretty woman from long ago.

When all parties were clear that this was not a police bust, and after Rai explained their purpose, the conversation turned efficient, even cordial.

"I know who to call," said the lead singer, whom Rai called "Taboo," but whose real name, it turned out, was Yochanan Reznick.

He disappeared into a side room and returned a few moments later. "I made some calls. They'll get back to me with answers in a bit."

He sat down and calmly looked at his visitors. Merlin studied him but didn't notice any change in his expression. *A kind of psychopath who just happened to find a nonviolent way to live,* Merlin thought.

"What was that song with the babies?" Zoe asked. "Because I go to lots of clubs and hear lots of crap, but I've never heard crap like this."

"It's metaphorical," said Taboo.

Rai gave her a "told you so" look.

"It's crap," Zoe determined.

Merlin looked at her desperately. They needed this guy's help. They needed his goodwill.

"Well, the clock is ticking, and we haven't got all day, right?" Taboo said. "Want to wait around and watch us play in the meantime?" He enjoyed seeing the horror spreading on the cop's face, then ordered his musicians, "Take a break. I'll play solo now." He turned to Merlin. "This won't be as terrible for you."

Taboo strapped on an acoustic guitar, the kind people use to play songs for their friends at the Sea of Galilee, and began singing slowly.

> "On this night the trees in the forest appear
> As the dead, alive in the moon and the snow
> Dreaming their lives . . . losing their minds as they
>   go . . ."

His phone rang.

"Lyrics by Uri Zvi Greenberg," he said and answered the call. He listened impassively for a few seconds, hung up, and told Merlin, "Initial results. The disabled man is called Eliyahu Selfter. His giant retarded son is Ephraim. Their address is 7 Rabbi Hazaz Street. They have a few regular routes. You can often find them on the Hashmonaim–King

George–Shenkin route, but not only there. Other people are going to get back to me soon."

"God, that was quick," Merlin said appreciatively.

Part of him wanted to pounce like a panther, dispatching forces and a warrant over to Rabbi Hazaz Street, but he knew he'd never be in this basement, with these people, ever again, and he had to know: *How?*

"The street knows," Yochanan Reznick, a.k.a., Taboo, explained. "I'm the street."

He thought about the door to the apartment of the third victim, Tamara Zelipowich. He had to go back to the crime scene. Something about that door. Something . . .

The police raided the empty apartment on Rabbi Hazaz, a tiny ground-floor place in a fine building in central Tel Aviv. Lots of household items, but no people, no incriminating evidence.

"I'm on my way," Merlin told them.

"This is cool. I'm coming with you," Zoe said.

Merlin reached his hand out to stop her, saying, "Listen, Zoe, your help up until this point has been nothing short of amazing, but I don't want you to get involved in this. Why don't we meet tomorrow morning and I'll update you . . . and consult with you. Tomorrow morning. What do you say?"

Zoe's eyes bugged out with shock. "Tomorrow morning? But I have school. I have to learn!"

"So let's put each other's numbers in our phones. I'm adding you now. It's a pact. Remember the way people used to prick their fingers and mix their blood? A pact, okay? I'll update you later today and see how you can help me out some more, all right?"

"Seriously? Have you ever mixed your blood with someone else's?"

He didn't answer. Her name was Dorit. There was a sandlot behind their school, along a low wall that ended in a field of mastic bushes. He ran into her two years ago in court. She was a lawyer.

"I'll update you, Zoe, I promise," he said with a smile.

"You deserve a kiss, Superintendent Jonah Merlin," Zoe said with a sweet smile. "Metaphorically speaking, of course."

———

The apartment on Hazaz Street wasn't much help. They spent three hours there and came up with zilch.

Merlin wandered the apartment slowly. A framed picture of a woman on a dresser in the foyer. The mirror behind it reflected the back of the photo and one word: "Rachel." Nothing but mundane objects sat inside the drawers. A tidy, modest kitchen. A living room with a sofa and some medical equipment. An outdated TV set. In the living room dresser, some phone books and receipt booklets for Selfter Locks—Door and Lock Experts.

"A locksmith . . . that could explain a few things," Merlin mumbled.

All around him, officers tapped the walls gently and methodically, searching for spaces, hiding places. One officer moaned from the dark, dusty crawl space.

The apartment had one small bedroom with two beds: a simple field cot covered with several blankets and a king-sized bed. The closet had a few clothes in it, all extra-large.

Captain Flint called Merlin into the bathroom. The medicine cabinet contained a lot of different pill bottles. Flint said, "Listen, I feel the same as you: they must have left. That's the vibe here. But there are a few things in this cabinet that you'd take with you if you were splitting. Either you have a second stash, or you take them with you."

"I've got a headache," said Merlin.

"Let's hope these really are the killers," Captain Flint sighed.

A few people walked into the apartment. One of them was Superintendent Eran Shatzki from the International Investigations Department—the head of the team formed in parallel to Merlin's.

"Hey, Jonah."

"Hey, Shatzki. Help yourselves. Just do it in a way that this killer's lawyers don't make fools of us later."

"These killers, plural. Got it."

"Killers. Listen, this headache is killing me. I'm going outside, Shatzki. If you find a body or a murderer, share that with me."

Merlin stepped out to the wet yard. A mean-looking puddle made him veer toward a concrete shelter containing gas tanks and trash cans. He glanced behind it, for no good reason. Later, he wouldn't be able to explain to himself why he'd pushed his way between the structure and the giant bush that grew on the wall that separated the yard from the adjacent one.

"Captain Flint!" he yelled. "Shatzki, get over here!"

A group of officers walked out into the yard.

"Welcome to the training grounds," said Merlin.

Like a pack of excited children, the officers pushed through to glance behind the concrete shelter. A red scrawl reading "And I shed tears of happiness and helplessness" glimmered alongside some other lettering.

"We've got them, huh?" Shatzki said, glowing.

"Other than the fact that we have no idea where they are, or if they're murdering the next victim as we speak, then yes, we've got them," said Superintendent Merlin.

Commander Menashe Bried was asked to come over. Before he even arrived, one of his in-house journalists showed up. Merlin texted Zoe with the pride of a skilled user: "Come." Rai Zitrin arrived before her. *What was going on between those two?*

"Rai, listen, I need you to save me," Merlin said gravely. "Take my credit card. I'll explain where to find the automatic ticketing machine. You just swipe the card through the slot, and you'll get four tickets. You're a lifesaver."

"Zoe will be here soon," Rai said and took the credit card. "She had a fight with her mom, or something."

The sun emerged in all its glory from behind a parade of black clouds that had finished pouring rain that morning but had yet to file out. The rays sprinkled sparkles on the green grass of the Tel Aviv yard.

"Captain Flint, come with me," said Merlin, walking to a point in the thick grass where there was an imperceptible line of missing weeds. "Get me a shovel or something."

A few moments later, they revealed the bunker: a large wooden box sunk into the earth, no handle. A small crack allowed the three men to pry it open. It took three men to open it, or one giant.

Inside the box were weapons, greased and wrapped.

"The resistance to the British Mandate in the Land of Israel, at your service," said Flint, picking up one of the weapons. "An antique. I don't know what it is. I'll call my expert."

Commander Bried entered the yard, along with six officers. Merlin had been surprised that none of the neighbors was watching them, but now heads began emerging from balconies all around. Then he saw the small bundle inside the box.

"Take it out, carefully," he told one of Flint's men.

A very old book, in Polish. He didn't need to read Polish to know the name of the author.

Merlin looked at the book and used his right hand to text Zoe: "Hurry."

CHAPTER 22

LITTLE ELIYAHU SELFTER WATCHES ADELA

Little Eliyahu Selfter is standing on the balcony, singing: "Speak of the heart of Jerusalem and call to it, for its armies are prepared, for its punishment has been served." He's nearly bar mitzvah age. The Tel Aviv sun transforms dust into a magic trick, and across the street Adela is mopping the floors again. The hot water sends intricate arabesques of steam into the air, like blooming letters, as if ancient books are rising to escape the floor. Little Eliyahu watches and sings: "For it has taken twice the punishment from God in penance for its sins . . ."

Two more months until his bar mitzvah. Two more months, and he still can't sing. His mother has arranged things with the rabbi, who agreed to come, as long as he could teach the boy his haftorah on the balcony. "Your apartment is hot like a punishment from hell," he said.

Eliyahu's mother was a little insulted. This is the apartment her friends arranged for her, and Eliyahu knows they have to be modest. After the Nazis murdered his father, good friends in Israel arranged a place for mother and only son to lay their heads. They helped his mother with everything, and sometimes even spent the night.

"Tonight you'll go to bed early, Eliyahu."

But his mother has arranged his bar mitzvah all on her own. She's taken care of everything. He just has to learn how to sing, but he can't do it. Downstairs, across the street, Adela steps out onto the balcony. She is old, but in her red dress and long hair she catches even the rabbi's eyes.

Tfu, spits the rabbi. *Sinful.*

Now they both lower their heads.

The sticky, sugary dust of May invades the streams of sunshine. Eliyahu Selfter sings thinly. He's afraid of the rabbi. What would he tell his mother? Within the glowing dust he sees armies, ghostly horsemen, mighty visions. Mother always tells him off: "You're always in your own imaginations, Eliyahu." She collects every coin she can, so they can survive. She has good friends. She has to beg a lot. Eliyahu doesn't like the friends. He lies awake in his room. He must fall asleep. It is imperative that he fall asleep. *But how?* Darkness pounces like a cat. Gray-black demons skip around on scarves. He imagines he can hear a song from afar. Forest witches singing in young Adela's voice. Her braids long, so long. His gaze lingers and lingers, lost in darkness. Little Eliyahu Selfter falls asleep.

The bar mitzvah is two months away. The guest list is short. He will sing: "He who sits on the land whose dwellers are like grasshoppers, who leans like the sky and stretches it like a tent under which to sit." They'll throw candy at him.

Adela stands on the balcony, leaning her arms on the scorching railing, her red smiles traveling upward, tickling little Eliyahu's flesh. *Tfu*, the rabbi spits.

——

He can still remember their neighbor Barney Landman running. Each time little Eliyahu Selfter looked down at the yard, he saw the frightening shadows of that moment. That evening. It was so long ago, and it keeps happening all the time. He heard whistles and muffled voices. He'd never heard gunshots before. Barney Landman rolling over the wall. His shirt red. Little Eliyahu watching with horror. The strong man crawling through the yard, among the weeds. Like a snake. Like a lizard. Eliyahu knows exactly where the scary neighbor is trying to get. The bunker. Little Eliyahu discovered it a long time ago. It's a secret. The strong man crawls, and the weeds behind him turn red. Green weeds with red edges. British officers appear. They jump over the wall. One more move for Barney, and he's surrounded. They look around. *Is anyone watching?* Little Eliyahu shivers. The British guns click. The sounds of the shots are frightening. And somewhat pleasant. Little Eliyahu doesn't see a thing. From his hiding place in the balcony closet he counts twelve explosions. The explosions end. He counts again and again. Twelve. Twelve. The Brits are going to shoot little Eliyahu. The Germans had already shot his father.

The officers shout in their language. All around, from balconies, people carefully peek out. No one saw what happened. Only Eliyahu. He creeps out of the closet on his stomach. Across the kitchen floor. He counts to twelve, counts to twelve over and over again, until he falls asleep.

———

After that red night, Barney's apartment remained empty and black. Only Eliyahu would follow what happened there. He saw cats walking in and never coming out. He saw pigeons landing on the railing and disappearing into shadow. Once he saw a thief sneak in and then leave immediately.

And one evening, his mother, in a nightgown, sits at the kitchen table, drinking tea and crushing a white pill in her mouth. The friend of that evening has left. His mother is crying, "I've been with geniuses,

Eliyahu. I've been with geniuses . . ." The sadness leaking from her eyes could fill all of Poland, drip into Ukraine, and submerge all the lands of evil.

"Go to sleep, Eliyahu."

Eliyahu sneaks out onto the balcony. The shadows are playing chess but ignoring the rules down there. The next morning, all of a sudden, in that black apartment downstairs windows, shutters, doors open. Warm water and soap. Brooms and brushes. Rags and cloths.

The neighbors explain: Barney Landman's wife has arrived. The apartment belongs to her. Her name is Adela.

Eliyahu's mother says, "Whore."

Eliyahu looks at Adela. She isn't young; she's old. Barney Landman, before he had to flee the Brits, always collected the prettiest whores from Café Lorentz. He always wore white suits, narrow shoes. He always held a foreign-brand cigarette. A criminal and an evil man.

Eliyahu watches. This Adela woman is old. Her dress looks like a robe. A girl his age is holding on to the dress. The neighbors explain: she's Adela, too.

———

Little Eliyahu sits at Café Lorentz. It's his first time. He doesn't know it is also his last.

A man with very smooth cheeks has come to their house and taken him and his mother in a nice car. He's an uncle, his mother told him. He's an uncle. At Café Lorentz, he is seated on a chair and served hot chocolate and a piece of cake. The uncle places a palm over Eliyahu's mother's small hand.

"Go look at the fountain, Eliyahu."

Inside the fountain, air bubbles float like pomegranate seeds in infinity, wandering in the water, mindless and happy.

Eliyahu's dark eyes wander, too. Across from him is an old man with an empty teacup. The sun fixes him with a long spear that dives from above through all the clouds. The old man won't see the end of summer. At a table by the small platform of the maître d' are three men in heavy woolen suits. Neither the sun, nor the sizzling air, nor the sweat beading on their pink necks will persuade them to remove their suit jackets, to loosen their ties. One of them looks over at Eliyahu's mother. Once. Twice.

May you be cursed with the black fire of Hitler's grave, may you die in the fire with Titus, Antiochus, Adrianus, the Mufti, the British detective Morton.

"Die," Eliyahu whispers. "Die."

CHAPTER 23

JONAH MERLIN GETS IN OVER HIS HEAD

Sometimes you knock on a door, a lock rattles, and a normal life appears. Nothing special. Other times, it's a kind of hell. This time it was neither.

After Jonah Merlin finished searching Eliyahu Selfter's apartment and ordered the officers and Shatzki's team to go to each apartment in the building, in case one of the neighbors knew something, he visited the next-door apartment. He assumed nobody was home. Dozens of police officers had been walking the halls for over an hour, making noise, speaking into their radios, and no one had glanced out of that apartment or asked any questions.

His hand slapped the door. The rattle of a lock and an older lady appeared at the doorway, her figure hovering over him like a portrait of his own mother.

"What do you want from Eliyahu?" she asked.

He stifled a gasp at her resemblance to his dead mother. He introduced himself, flashed his badge, and asked to speak to her inside.

"Ever since my husband, Shmuel, passed away, I don't let anyone inside," she said, remaining planted in her place.

Officers walked up and down the stairs, occasionally calling something to him. He looked at the woman. Her name was Nitza Ardan, according to the small plaque by the doorbell. He'd ask her a couple questions and move on.

"I don't know anything," she said, beating him to the punch. "I haven't spoken to Eliyahu in about ten years, and neither did my husband Shmuel, before he died. But you won't hear a bad word about Eliyahu from me!"

"Why don't you speak to him?"

"You know how it is . . . you're neighbors for years; one day one of you says something, and you don't talk anymore. Like that. He's a hard man, Eliyahu, but you won't hear a bad word about him from me. How he stayed with a boy like that, raising him alone. You know what it's like to be alone with a boy like that? Eliyahu stayed. He never went with anyone else after his wife died."

If only Merlin could ask his mother if she happened to know this woman. *Maybe they were distant relatives?*

"There was a time, you know, when all sorts of ladies were sniffing around him. They thought, *A handsome man and he's got his own apartment; he's got potential.* But with a boy like Ephraim . . . What do *you* think? They gave up. All the ladies. He stayed alone with him, doing everything on his own, with a boy like Ephraim. Imagine what that must be like. Who would want him?"

"Ma'am, do you have any idea where he is now?"

"I told you, we haven't spoken in ten years."

"Did anyone come to help? Lend a hand? A boy like that, living with a man in a wheelchair."

"Sometimes he gave orders to the madman from the roof apartment. It used to be a laundry room, but it was illegally converted into a studio apartment. That wild savage moved in there a few years ago. No one speaks to *him*, either. An old man who wears a swimsuit in summer. Have you ever heard of anything like that, Mister Officer?"

Merlin began to say, "Thank you, Ma'am. Maybe just one more . . . ," but Mrs. Nitza Ardan was already swallowed back into her apartment. Merlin quickly took the stairs down, a knot in his chest. He stood outside in front of the mailboxes. The top one read, in smudged letters: "ASG Management."

A man in a wheelchair, a giant pushing him, and a third guy . . .

He dialed a number.

"Hey, Vadim, ASG Management—isn't that the company that booked Eliyahu Selfter's hotel? The one owned by Shimshon Krieker?"

CHAPTER 24

SHIMSHON KRIEKER

He was born in 1940, an eldest child, in one of the villages of the Hula Valley. His mother died giving birth to him. His father, a party member and a politico, named him Shimshon. Because he was born prematurely, and feeble, and because compromise was his father's specialty, Shimshon's father strived to meet reality halfway, somewhere between the heroic name—the Hebrew version of Samson—and the infant crying meekly in his crib, his limbs spindly and his lips blue. At first, Shimshon was considered an original wonder in the young village, but soon new children were born, beating him in every accomplishment, and the contours of his wretchedness were redrawn anew each day. Often, for no reason at all, the children hit him, abusing him with cruel ceremony. Even his half brother, Giora, three years younger than him, participated, his enthusiasm exceeding that of their peers. When Shimshon began to go to school, his achievements were meager, a humiliation to his father. He was told in no uncertain terms that he wasn't trying, wasn't making an effort, and that he was bringing everyone else down with him.

Only one place always belonged to him: the lake. When he started swimming in the water of the Hula Lake, his superiority was revealed for the first time. It was hard to truly swim in the lake. The endeavor involved maneuvering through thickets of reeds, and it turned out that the children who were more muscular and flexible than he were no better in navigating the waters.

Shimshon liked to disappear for long stretches of time among the shadows and the decay of the mysterious banks. He floated like soft steam on the surface of the brown water and then dove into the unmoving rot. From the moment he dove down, hearing the meaningless sound of the water's babbling, it was as if he'd vanished, recovering his senses, thoughts bursting into his mind. Thoughts of grandeur. Of heroism. Of supremacy. When he raised his head out of the water, looking straight into the sun, in blindness or victory, his mind brimmed with colorful images, all resembling the small rug his father brought back from some political tour of faraway Mexico, its fragile patterns vivid and tangled and wild.

He suffered every day. He felt his torment every hour on the hour. There was always someone around to further excruciate him. His worst moments were always caused by that one older man who recognized his loneliness and took him among the tamarisk trees at nights, hurting him. When he was ten years old, his father was appointed to a senior role in some Tel Aviv organization, and he was uprooted and moved to the city. His head was hollow, his thoughts scattered. He had neither friends nor accomplishments. He missed the babbling of water. Any chance he had, he ran away from school, finding bushes to hide among and from which to look into the sun, right into it, until the Mexican rugs swirled within him and he passed out.

The doctors diagnosed epilepsy.

But he knew it was self-induced, and that he would heal when he wanted to.

He hated the city, its streets, the roaring, the long walls of bright white houses. One day, his wandering led him to a deep winter puddle at the edge of the city, muddy and crowded with vegetation, near the Ayalon Stream. From that point on, each day, after pretending to walk to school at a safe distance from the other children, he turned and headed to the pond instead. Every winter day, he walked into his pond, swam in the frigid water, and disappeared in the reeds. The rumors of the small ghost that lived in the puddle reached the ears of many, as did stories of a boy who'd been drowned there a century earlier, of a groom who'd been searching for his bride in the pond for the past 250 years, of a hyena-like demon crawling through the pond on its stomach.

One time, as he dove into his winter pond, his half brother, Giora, who'd followed him there, stole his clothes. Shimshon had to go home naked. After that, his father could no longer take the looks the neighbors gave him on the street. Shimshon was punished harshly, and his father resented him, because lashing a child with a belt was an ideological contradiction of everything he stood for.

At the time, his father was transferred to a position in the Water Department, working under the famous engineer Klievanov, and was meant to become a member of the group in charge of the miraculous drying of the Hula Lake. All his energy was harnessed to the national project, and Shimshon was left behind, along with his half brother and stepmother. Shimshon heard that, far away, in his place of birth, his childhood lake was being drained and dried up, and that his father was the one doing the deed. As his bar mitzvah approached, his winter pond in Tel Aviv was also being dried, as part of the conquering and taming of the entire Ayalon Stream.

Like everybody else his age, Shimshon was a member of a youth movement. On the first night of a field trip he sat alone, staring at the fire. He was familiar with the duel between the blinding flame and his eyes, and he watched the fire until he found himself inside a vision. He saw the fire crawling toward him. The circle of stones remained black and empty, and the fire slowly grew nearer, climbing heavily toward him, enveloping him and penetrating him through every opening. When he awoke at the hospital, he found his father dozing off in a chair by his side, two days' worth of stubble on his cheeks. His youth movement guide was standing at his bedside. He looked at Shimshon and said plainly, "You just slept for two days."

After that, he was asked to refrain from joining trips. Not required, just asked. From that day on he accompanied the trips from a distance, crawling surreptitiously behind the row of children during the day, erecting a hidden camp not far from his merry friends at night. He would take his revenge, sneaking into the camp and stealing all the candy that had been prepared as a surprise for the happy campers, or destroying a structure built with sweat. He was never caught, never seen, never suspected. Shimshon began viewing himself as a commando warrior.

In the meantime, he became an orphan. Just another routine Syrian shelling aimed at the driers of the Hula Lake, which, this time, took his father's life, among the forty anonymous men who were killed—the price of their lives forgotten by history. Shimshon remained with only his stepmother and his half brother, Giora, and the world quickly stopped taking an interest in him, limiting him, not demanding he achieve anything.

The year his father died, Shimshon discovered the sea. He tested his strength by swimming ever longer distances. He loved the moments when he was very far away from the beach, calculating his energy: If I swim one more meter, I can still make it back to the beach. Another meter—yes, I can still do it. One more meter—not sure. And then another. Too far . . . I've gone too far. One more meter. Now turn around. Sometimes he barely managed to stagger onto the shore, heaving, pale, imagining what would have happened had he dared swim a little farther out to sea. He promised himself to try it next time. One time, a school of fins crossed his path, and he couldn't tell if they belonged to dolphins or sharks. One rubbed up against him, fast as lightning. Shark? Dolphin? He knew only this: that light touch gave him the powers of the sea creature.

He would be a naval commando warrior.

In summer, the sea churned with people. Rude, ugly, loud, mean. Instead of the beach, his legs pulled him toward the roaring lions at the Tel Aviv Zoo. In return for the help he offered, zookeepers allowed him to wander freely among the animals. Unlike the screaming children, excited by the games of monkeys or the hopping flamingoes, Shimshon knew his task was to acquire the animals' powers. He stopped, silent, in front of each and every cage, caught the animals' eyes and had a staring contest.

He only grew tired of the zoo after having defeated his most stubborn opponent, a male lion in his large cage. Many times, the battle had ended with Shimshon giving in to the lion, who fixed him with his indifferent, determined eyes, while Shimshon's body grew weak and his eyes burned with pain. But eventually, one day, when the zoo was about to close, their eyes locked to the point of pain, and suddenly the mighty lion bent his body, closed his eyes for a moment, and lost his power to little Shimshon.

Shimshon passed out in front of the cage. Someone carried him home. But from that day on he knew he was the mightiest of the mighty, a king, immune from all injuries.

When he turned eighteen, he wanted to join the naval commandos. The doctors rejected him.

One stormy night he snuck past security, invading the naval commando base, and waited for the base commander in his office. The commander was alarmed, taken aback; he searched for his weapon. From behind the slammed door he negotiated with the strange civilian, who wanted only one thing: to enlist in the commandos. The backup force that had been called captured the civilian and handed him over to the police. Shimshon did not resist. A week later, early in the morning, the commander arrived at his office to find Shimshon again, wet and shivering, and demanding to be accepted into the naval commandos. The commander sent Shimshon away without a commitment, and alerted all unit soldiers that if anyone ever managed to break through the security cordons and enter his office again all leaves, ceremonies, parties, and promotions would be canceled for a year. A few days later, as he opened the door to his office, he could already smell the odor of a man wet with the water of the sea, and he knew—Shimshon had won. He sent a telegram to the induction center, in which he demanded: draft the boy into my unit.

Shimshon's training went without a hitch. He excelled in every field and was assigned a unit. No one could swim or dive like he could. And once he permitted his body the right to madness, no one had his cruelty or crazy aggression.

When he was assigned to train for a first special operation, he found himself refusing. They wanted him to kill people. He didn't want to do that.

"What do you mean, 'No'?"

"No."

"But that's part of the job. That's the goal. Not that we like doing it."

He'd agree to do it, but only on condition that he know the people he killed, end of story.

Just as he'd been accepted beyond the letter of the law, so was he discharged, with a handshake, and disappeared into the lap of civilian life. He worked on fishing boats, in orchards, in factories. One day his former commander made him an offer: he could be a commando, but in order to save, rather than take, a life. He was assigned to the secret project of bringing Moroccan Jews to Israel. For several years, he worked among the people who assisted in naval immigrant operations, and during this time he met the new immigrant Esther.

"Do you believe me when I say a fire entered me?"

"Yes."

"Do you believe my body was merged with the body of a lion at the zoo?"

"Yes."

"Do you believe a strong sea creature transferred its powers to me?"

"Yes."

They had seven children.

Shimshon completed his work on the immigration of Moroccan Jews shortly before the shoddy ship, named *Nut* by someone with a terribly prophetic sense of humor, drowned at sea. People from a clandestine department of the Jewish Agency asked him to work with them, this time assisting the Jews of the Soviet Union. They wanted him to be one of the few and anonymous people who maintained a tenuous relationship between the State of Israel and the Jewish community captured in the Soviet state. Shimshon accepted.

Once he traveled to the south of the USSR, and when he saw the Volga River, its enormous tangles and the muddy earth sprawling on both its banks like an endless shimmering carpet, he decided to ask the Soviet government to allow him to migrate to their country, and make his home along the Volga. People in stiff suits discussed his request. He was asked to contribute to the country that was taking him and his family in, meaning, to betray; meaning, to become a double agent, working for the Soviet secret service. Shimshon accepted.

In spite of his faith in his special powers, Shimshon was not a talented spy. After several small and failed missions, some people in stiff suits approached him with an offer: travel with his Israeli passport to Belgium and take out a man, an enemy of the Soviet people. Shimshon accepted, with one caveat: "I want to get to know him first. I have to."

The deal was struck. He went to Belgium and befriended the target of his mission. He had no idea that Soviet embassy attachés were following him. He also had no idea that Israeli Intelligence had caught wind of his doings. Three weeks after meeting his victim, he left him, lifeless, in a Brussels hotel room and returned to Russia.

Israeli Intelligence exposed his connections to the Soviets, and when it became clear he would not be able to return to Israel, he was allowed to stay and live in an impoverished village hugged by the Volga River, as a Soviet citizen. He lived in the Russian village of Zulfena for thirty years, not allowed to leave its confines. He didn't want to leave his Volga, anyway. His wife, Esther, passed away. Two of his children died from disease. The other five scattered all around the globe. He lived alone by the Volga, drawing from its strength, giving it his. No one interrupted his hermit lifestyle. No one took an interest.

In 1991, he heard of the waves of Russian immigration to Israel. He wanted to join. He waited.

One day a Jew from Moscow arrived at his village, interested in purchasing some factories in the area. He was sharp-minded and quick of hand, one of those people who, upon the collapse of the great Soviet empire, snatched up factories from the Soviet people, to be held in their privatized hands. His name was Samson Krieker.

He needed a guide and a guard, and Shimshon offered his services, free of charge, from one Jew to another.

"I'd like to get to know you," Shimshon told him.

"Don't worry. Do your job properly, and you'll be in my book," Samson Krieker said with a wink. He was used to sycophants and helpers and thought he might find a way to reward this strange Volgan type, too.

Two weeks later, coiffed and clean-shaven, wearing fine clothing, Shimshon Krieker flew to Israel along with his new name, carrying Samson's passport, as its original owner, cut into pieces and strewn among the bushes on the banks of the Volga, awaited the resurrection.

———

Shimshon Krieker spent almost twenty years in isolation in Israel, living on the outskirts of reality, on the margins of activity. He made no friends, and spent many days swimming in the streams that were warm even in winter, and in the blue sea, whose wonderful shimmering expanse he'd already forgotten. He was an older man, silent and lonesome.

He happened to walk down the street where the commotion took place that day. An ambulance, a police car, and dozens of curious onlookers. Someone had fallen from a roof. Shimshon Krieker approached. Rather than keeping away from people, from crowds, from chatter, he was drawn in, and for some reason a path was cleared for him. He wasn't stopped. He got all the way to the man lying on the stretcher, grinding his teeth, and his eyes met those odd eyes for the first time.

Like the eyes of the lion, like the fin of the dolphin, like the flames rising and climbing from the bonfire.

The man, who appeared erect even when lying down with a broken back, summoned him with his finger, gave him a ring of keys and, calmly, his voice hovering above the excruciating pain and the hellish agony, whispered an address and instructed him, "Go there. There's a boy alone in the apartment. Take care of him until I get back. I will repay you."

Shimshon Krieker knew that someone had conquered all of his powers. It was as if he'd been ravaged. He knew he would carry out this man's irrational orders.

He went to the address given him in order to take care of the boy in the apartment. And from that moment on, Shimshon Krieker swore to obey Eliyahu Selfter until the day he died.

CHAPTER 25

CONNECTIONS ARE REVEALED

Commander Menashe Bried never had an original idea in his life. Not one. But he was always a good listener, knowing what to publicize. He absorbed the ideas of others and bankrolled them in important meetings, at the right moment, trying them out in small hallway chats, writing them in notes to high-ranking officials, succinctly and efficiently. As a matter of principle he always cited his sources. He opened by saying, "Eli had an idea," or "I heard it from Merlin and thought his idea was worth considering." His ironclad rule was to mention the original owner of the idea five or six times, until every last listener realized how hard Commander Bried was trying to give credit, forced as it may be, to another, and a thought formed naturally in their minds: the idea is Bried's, but he has an interest in talking up the person he keeps mentioning.

Now he stood on a small podium, in front of dozens of microphones and cameras, playing his famous piece entitled "We are making every possible effort."

The headlines in newspapers and websites seemed to emerge even as the reporters stood in front of Commander Bried like a roaring wall of lava. A spontaneous hatching, a creation from the bits of information provided by Bried, from the deluge of questions poured out by reporters, brewing a storm within itself, until the crumbs of letters flew up into the atmosphere to become headlines, updates, articles, photo captions.

Commander Bried was satisfied.

"We're prepared once more to return safety to the citizens of Tel Aviv and the entire country."

He was talking about the second investigation team, led by Superintendent Eran Shatzki. Several times that day a hostile delivery-man arrived at the station to transfer materials from Merlin's team to Shatzki's team. Shatzki himself had spoken to Merlin three times.

Commander Menashe Bried said, "We're utilizing an international relations protocol that makes the best of the synergy of a pan-national system collaboration." He was referring to a short fax received at the station, which contained one laconic English statement: "No available information was found regarding missing person Keynan Levin."

He said, "The citizens of Tel Aviv, the Dan region, and the State of Israel can feel safe again."

It was unclear what he meant.

At the same time, Merlin sat silently with his two teammates in a conference room that had been cleared out for them. Piles of reports rested on the table, some neatly stacked and some strewn into layers of scattered paper, marked with pen and with Tal's magic markers. The three of them were concentrating on a careful reading. Once in a while Kelsitz snorted with contempt in light of a factoid acquired not by pointing a gun to someone's head. Tal's gaze got lost from time to time in the window facing west. Merlin guessed that her professional thoughts were mixing with moments of hatred toward men, things she would later tell her lawyer, thoughts as glittering as pins about a checkup for Kid A or a tetanus shot for Kid B or C. Outside, the sun was abundant. It was a glowing, cloudless afternoon, which seemed suspicious, as if hiding an approaching storm, another European cold front to stride like a violent army into the defenseless atmosphere of Israel, striking with polite, sophisticated European viciousness. The Spanish Cortés on his way to the Inca castle.

Superintendent Merlin rubbed his eyes. *Afternoon.* He'd already spoken to Hadas.

Where was Zoe right now? He tried to imagine her at a school desk, her long legs crossed at the ankles, her eyes fixed on the teacher and the blackboard.

On his way from the empty apartment on Hazaz Street back to the police station, he'd stopped at the light and watched two schoolgirls in flip-flops, shorts, and tank tops crossing the sunny street, sweat-shirts wrapped around their shoulders in case the weather changed. He looked at their bare legs, their tight calves, the muscles rising perfectly to the knees, and then branching to form flawless thighs. One girl's top exposed a patch of tight, tan belly above her pants, featuring a small, curvy, pubescent paunch. He watched the beautiful feet. He wanted to throw himself at those feet, to kiss them.

"You're an idiot." That's what Merlin had told himself at the traffic light, and that's what he was telling himself now. "You're an idiot."

Kelsitz snorted in protest and slammed his fist onto a thin stack of papers. He summarized his research, regarding a possible familial relation between Tamara Zelipowich and the cousins Levin.

"Well, *nu*, not relatives. We're all Jewish, except for those of us who have trouble with the Chief Rabbinate, but we're not all family. My family got to enjoy the Law of Return only because we all have ugly noses. The birth certificates we brought back from there? The Israeli government spat on them. And my father dared argue, because of his honor. Mom told him not to say anything. To this day he claims that not only is he Jewish, but that his father was born in Israel, in the Hula Valley. It's a good thing Mom shut him up." Kelsitz glanced at his audience. Both members were looking at their documents. "Okay, I'm going to take a walk. Even prisoners are allowed that. Shawarma, anyone?"

Tal raised her beautiful eyes.

One day, Kelsitz would make a terrific rebellion instigator. He knew just which cracks to slip the knife into.

"Forty-minute break," Merlin said, giving in. "And then back to work. The murderer doesn't take breaks."

"He doesn't read documents, either," said Kelsitz, already on his way out into the sun.

Merlin stayed in his seat. He dialed a number on his phone.

"It's about tickets to your show," he said. "Are they only valid in Tel Aviv? If I take my kids to Ashkelon, can I use them there?"

That morning, at the hospital, Kelsitz visited the bedside of the screaming driver, who'd complained that after his jeep crushed the Fiat, three people got out of their car, told him they weren't there to help, that he deserved to die, and stopped others from helping. One in a wheelchair, one giant, and a third man.

Kelsitz returned with no results, explaining to Merlin, "I wasted an hour there; couldn't get anything out of him. If you'll let me go back privately . . . No? Because he wants a deal. He thinks he deserves applause for crossing into another lane line while speeding on a rainy night and killing two people, only because he remembers something that might be important. Trust me, Jonah, if I go back privately, he'll spill. What do you say?"

Merlin's face remained expressionless.

Kelsitz moaned and twisted his face with disgust, saying, "I don't like rules. I like order. I like discipline. Yes. But rules? Blat."

Merlin felt a chill. *Go privately.* The words reminded him of his parents whispering in the kitchen at night when his mother was very sick. She whispered to his father what the doctor had insinuated: If they paid, he'd see them privately. If they came privately, a different procedure might become available. His parents calculated their funds, checking their accounts this way and that, and little Jonah got out of his bed for a sip of water and looked at the dining table, strewn with pencils and notepads. His father said, "Yes, at any price." His mother said, "It won't help; you'll need the money later." Jonah listened from bed. They never did end up going.

It was strange, to sit at a desk, reading documents. To sift, to investigate, while all the while something in his soul called on him to act, to charge, to perform. *But what?* All the police stations in the country—and the public, too, actually—had received an alert regarding a man in a wheelchair and a giant at his side, and possibly a third person. *How long could such a circus-like pack stay under the radar?*

Merlin called Superintendent Dido Partuk.

"What's going on? Is she all right?"

Superintendent Partuk informed him that everything was fine, but he sounded strange, a little confused. *What was going on down there?*

They exchanged a few sentences regarding the purpose of guarding Gili Levin. Merlin admitted that he wasn't sure she was even a target. There had been an arrow pointing in her direction, but now it wasn't so clear anymore. Dido Partuk expressed his chagrin about the thankless job. As far as he was concerned, Gili Levin was a depressed, vegan Buddhist anarchist. And the worst part, the poor cell reception down there.

"Even the police Motorola keeps going *zzzzsssshhhh*."

"But we're agreed that you'll stay there for now, right?"

"You know, Merlin, on the one hand a serial killer just took out two of her cousins. That's a reason to protect her, for sure. On the other hand, you're still not sure it wasn't *her* who took *them* out. Great. Down here, with all this quiet and desert, a thought came to me. You know what I think, Merlin? That as much as I love you, I have a station to run, too, and I need to get a move on."

"Are you bringing in a replacement, Partuk? Because you're the only one I trust."

"That's what I've been getting at, Merlin. I'm leaving tomorrow, day after tomorrow at the latest. I'll leave one of my guys here. Listen, I have a boss, too."

"Partuk, listen. I understand the pressure. We'll figure something out. Hold on . . . listen. On the one hand, our information doesn't show her to be the obvious next victim. On the other hand, my intuition tells me that someone needs to be with her."

"So?"

"Someone *good* needs to be with her."

"So?"

Kelsitz walked back into the conference room, glanced disgustedly at the reports, and put his fists to his temples.

"I'll send someone down immediately. One of my field men," Merlin said cheerfully. "You'll love him, Partuk. Just . . . don't beat each other up."

Merlin hoped he wasn't completely wrong. He couldn't really explain to his supervisors why that lady down in the desert needed such heavy protection, and why, of all people, Kelsitz was the guy for the job. He thought about Zoe. She was insulted. Well, that wasn't what he should be worrying about right now. She was a confused seventeen-year-old. *What did she want? To be part of the investigation? Part of the action?* After she'd arrived at the apartment on Hazaz Street, and translated the Polish, and showed everyone that the lines marked in the book were the exact ones to appear at the crime scenes, he thanked her and asked her to leave. Those kinds of things didn't just end with an arrest. He didn't want her in a place that was going to see extreme violence. That's what he told her.

"I don't want you in a place that's going to see extreme violence. I don't want you to see anything horrific. Understand?"

"You're right. That's why I never go into the bathroom at school."

"Zoe, enough. Be a grown-up and realize . . ."

"You're kicking me out. I've done my part and now . . ."

"Zoe . . ."

"Drop it. Once again Zoe Navon trusted the wrong man. Congratulations, that's the one-hundredth man in your short life, Zoe—you deserve a gift."

He tried to say more, but she turned around uncooperatively, moving away.

"Zoe, really . . ."

She screamed, "I deserve a gift! And I'm going to buy it with coupons!"

Jonah glanced around. All the officers' eyes were on him.

Superintendent Eli Levy burst into the quiet room, and Merlin looked up.

"Limor," Merlin called. "Mazel tov! She had the baby!"

Levy twisted his mouth in dismissal, returning to the matter at hand.

"Listen, Merlin, listen. I just realized what's been bugging my memory this whole time. Listen. That victim, the new one, Zelipowich? Remember how we laughed? You don't remember her? A few years ago, she filed a series of complaints about her neighbor. She said she was a witch, that she was unnatural. That she was a whore."

Merlin tapped a finger to his forehead and said, "Oh man, I remember. Greeman, wasn't it, the one who filed her complaint? The door at the crime scene . . . there was something about the door that bugged me. It was her name. I knew I'd seen it before."

"Here, look," Levy said, handing his colleague a stack of papers. "I've come to move your investigation forward. It's from the police computer system. A complaint about the neighbor across the street. She accused her of black magic and prostitution."

"Did she suggest burning her at the stake?"

"Pretty much."

"So what does that have to do with us?"

"I don't know."

"Okay, look, I already feel like an idiot as it is," said Merlin. "I'm sitting here, while who knows where that trio is running around. No one can find them. They just can't. How can a group like that just disappear? And, of course, a man in a wheelchair was already beaten up on the street in Bat Yam. So I don't think the issue with the neighbor is too urgent right now."

"By the way, she wasn't completely wrong, your victim. That neighbor, she really did run some sort of whorehouse. She wasn't really . . . she would host old people—a small, select group of clients. They didn't just come in to sleep with her. She cooked for them, all sorts of delicacies they missed from the past, from the old days. She would go shopping and prepare the meal they wanted. They came over at night, dressed up like nobility. She was a true lady. They ate together, and then they went to bed. A small, select group of clients. That was it. When we went to check on her, she was gone. Just like that. Left her apartment, left everything. Evaporated. The neighbors who had complained went on to complain about new things. A few old men became lonelier. Sadder. That was the whole story."

"Levy, what are we doing? The entire Israel Police force is on alert in case those three pop up. Dido Partuk is on Gili Levin's tail, and I sent Vadim over to join him. And the next victim might be someone else altogether. We have no idea why he killed that Zelipowich. And you saw for yourself—there was hate there. He murdered her with so much hate."

Superintendent Eli Levy, who would soon become police commissioner, patted Merlin's back.

"Listen, I should get going. I came to help, and now I'm out of here. Going home, to Limor. Call me if you want to hear how jealous I am."

"You know if Shatzki's any closer? Does he have any leads?"

"No. But he's a good guy. He only works with cops. People have been saying you've found a young girl and a gay guy to partner up with."

"He isn't gay. And even if he is, show some respect. Be enlightened, at least around me."

"So, enlightened man, did you do any googling this morning?"

"I'm dead tired, Eli, and I think this is where the critical period begins. I think he's about to do his grand finale. He left his house and he's going on his final job. That's what it looks like."

He called Hadas and swallowed down a cold vending machine sandwich. As he spoke to her, he glanced distractedly at the pile of papers produced by the police computer—the late Tamara Zelipowich's contact with law enforcement authorities. Hadas cheered him up, promising him all sorts of treats just as he picked up a piece of paper that looked different from Tamara's other complaints: A man had walked into her apartment, gone berserk, and did some damage. This was a man who had tried to buy her apartment for a long time, using all sorts of tactics. The late Tamara Zelipowich detailed each object that had been broken or damaged, and finished with the declaration, "What happened to him afterward wasn't my fault, and he deserved it."

"Are you with me?" Hadas asked.

"I'll call you back, love."

Merlin hung up and looked at the paper. It seemed that after the man, Eliyahu Selfter, went wild in Tamara's apartment, he went up to the roof of the building and fell off. The fall crippled him. While the complaint was filed, he was still in rehabilitation at Tel HaShomer Hospital. Three years ago . . . Eliyahu Selfter . . . a hate crime . . .

Superintendent Eli Levy appeared in the hallway again, this time very slowly accompanying an old man with blue eyes and a white beard. A very ancient old man. A middle-aged woman walked beside him. Merlin's first thought was *She's so pretty.*

Levy announced, "Well, I wasn't able to go home just yet. Look who I have here for you. Sigal Levin-Halevy, Ronit's mother, Keynan's mother."

Merlin's eyes roamed from the beautiful woman to the old man, his colors so clear.

"This is my husband," said Sigal Levin, and a kind of determination, the strength she'd gathered, only broke as she mumbled at Merlin, "I just heard . . . Ronit . . . Keynan? They only told me today."

He offered her a seat. Offered one to the old man, too. Sigal shook her head no.

"I came to give you a letter. Keynan sent it to Ronit, but he must have gotten the address wrong, and it ended up in my mailbox. I didn't open it. I thought . . . I'd see her again . . . Ronit. Now I want you to read it."

"Sit. Would you like something to drink? Eat? Need a rest?"

They shook their heads. The sage remained standing, leaning on Levy's arm.

Merlin began to read the letter. A few moments later he raised his eyes.

"Gili Levin. She's going to be murdered. Soon. Quickly, we have to get every possible unit down there."

CHAPTER 26

A LETTER FROM KEYNAN LEVIN, THE FIRST
VICTIM, AS IT TURNS OUT

Dear Ronit, my kind sister, you sweet, vicious bitch,

By the time you read this letter, I'll be dead. Not just dead, murdered. For real, just like on television. Don't be sad, Ronit, my beloved sister, because as far as I'm concerned, something's finally happening at the right time. I'm writing you for a completely different reason—something terrible I've recently found out, and I didn't know whether to tell you, but now I think you have to know, you can't not know, and maybe knowing would help you clean yourself up, even just a little bit, from the dirt that every member of our family carries inside, in our souls, the dirt that's made us crooked and miserable. It's about our grandfather, Dr. Levin. You can just skip to the end now and get through with it, but if you still have a bit of love for your brother, who always tried to be nice, then read everything, linger with me at the stations of my life, even if some of them are just small and pathetic.

I've never been able to figure out what went wrong with me. How I got to be the way I am. I've spent twenty years living with partners who've admonished me: "How can you talk that way? Throughout history, we've fought for our right to be acknowledged just as we are— how dare you speak like our most primitive enemy? Like some sort of redneck, paving roads in Tennessee?" Oh well, some of my partners knew that rednecks sometimes make the best lovers.

That's just how it is. I'm a homo who thinks a family is a man-father and a woman-mother. And kids. And Mommy and Daddy love their kids. Not that I've ever met any family like that. So what? So I read Foucault and agreed with every word he wrote. I got used to living among people who condemned me, either directly or indirectly, for how my sexuality didn't contribute to society, but lately even some of my gay friends have been doing that. I've heard they were getting to be that way in Israel, too. Always trying to show how normal they are. Starting bourgeois families, raising kids, sighing about the price of preschool. Ridiculous. I adore Marcel Proust. He was right. We're a separate race. Sodomites. And oh, how I love it! I'm sure after Proust wrote about the "cursed race" through tearful eyes, he sighed indulgently, those same eyes glowing with spiteful French meanness . . . I should have moved to Paris, not here. But it's too late.

As if I'd have accomplished anything in Paris. I've always lived on a parabola that moves around my talents, keeping every point in my life at an equal distance between success and happiness. Otherwise, I would have been a math professor at the Hebrew University, not an impoverished, illegal alien with a persistent leg infection and an imminent end. Very imminent.

Funny, isn't it? My end is near, and it isn't even because of the infection. The infection came too late. As severe as it is, advancing deeper inside of me, it won't be administering the final blow. Something else is about to beat it to the punch. The contest for my soul has been decided. Funny, but in the time I still have left, the infection will give flesh to my suffering, a shape to my tragedy.

The end of life. And I've done nothing.

All the painkillers they gave me at Nathan Smith won't dull the sense that this infection got me because I invited it, the way you invite friends over for a movie and some pizza. Oh, that moment the pizza guy climbs the stairs, about to knock on the door, and you still have no idea—is it going to be a fat Hispanic guy with furry eyebrows, or a young guy with a smile like Liam Payne's? This infection is slow, relentless. For six months it's been burrowing through my left leg, and suddenly this Shimshon Krieker comes along, this bad liar, and is going to kill me. Some weird old man from Israel who's taken on an undercover mission that's a few sizes too big for him. Had I, the victim, not been so forgiving, he would have been locked up on Rikers long ago.

Kill me . . .

Want to? Go ahead.

He's been hanging around me for two weeks, telling me stories. "I'm a businessman from Israel looking for business opportunities, wanting to buy factories in the area." Oh, please. I guess no one's ever told him that when you meet such an extroverted homo, such an eternal candidate for abuse by all sorts of perverts and creeps, the guy has got some sensors, warning him of bad intentions from a thousand miles away.

Not that I've always said no to those kinds of intentions.

This time, it's going to be different. Let him kill me. After what I just found out—let him kill me.

I wonder . . . why hasn't he done it yet? The first time we met, as if by accident, he smiled and said, "I want to get to know you." Idiot. We've been hanging out for two weeks. And yesterday, completely by chance, I found out something that makes death a lot more desirable. So let him kill me.

I'm babbling, Ronit, because I want to write something, but I don't know how to get to it. Everything I've learned about the optimization of nonlinear, non-reentrant problems can't help me solve this one simple thing—how to write to you about the matter for which I'm writing. How many letters have I written you in my lifetime? Zero. Maybe a postcard, once, when I went to Rome on my first trip abroad after the army. So please, Ronit, patience, because this letter is important for your life, and I hope it's a good, wonderful, successful, long life.

Not like mine.

You're focused, efficient, goal-oriented. That's good. You'll accomplish things. Great things. With your boutique, and everything else. Not like me. You know what it's like to be able to read the most advanced math books the human mind could have composed, easily, simply, and never dare show up for an exam? To advise an architect boyfriend for three years, planning groundbreaking combinations of gorgeous designs with crucial calculations for him, and not be able to finish freshman year at the worst architecture school?

Well, Ronit. On this life journey, we both had the opportunity to be the children of Sigal Levin, the supermodel, the delicate beauty who gave me her beautiful features and the figure that made many women want to cut off parts of their flesh. Thanks, Mom, it helped me find guardian angels all these years. Thank you.

But you know, Ronit, I was Mom's outcast. From the day I was born. Grandma raised me. Mom turned away from me. She had no problem with you, and certainly not with Iris. She loved the two of you so much, with every fiber of her messed-up, doll-like being. It was only with me that things didn't work out, in spite of everyone's best attempts. Was it because of my penis, Mom? Was that all it was? A penis?

Grandma raised me. Frau Levin. So what if she was born Naomi Valero, a pure-blooded Sephardic Jew from Jerusalem? She was chosen by Dr. Levin to be his submissive wife, and ever since, that was it, she was Frau Levin. Wait, Ronit, this entire letter is going to converge on our grandfather, the venerable Dr. Andreas Levin. That terrible man. Just do me a favor. After you read this letter, go to his portrait that hangs by the management offices at the hospital, alongside the portraits of other past managers, and spit on it. Oh right, you're a lady. Don't spit, then; just put a dainty lighter to it and let it burn.

He married Grandma so she could serve him and all his uncontrollable needs. In the closed world of his mind, he must have believed he was gaining nobility points for taking in someone from a lower class, a

Mizrahi woman. But it's obvious to me that—just like in Escher's wonderful artwork—Grandma was also slumming it with him. She lowered herself from her high position to his. And he, Dr. Levin, Professor Levin, spent his entire life abusing her.

I started med school once, too, remember? My college entry exam scores allowed me to study anything I wanted. Maybe I wanted to follow in my genius grandfather's footsteps so that Mom might love me. Fucking subconscious. What was I thinking? I couldn't put anything together. Even when she once told me, just in passing, as if out of nowhere, that some people become doctors to save people from suffering, some care about science, while for others it's simply the best way to control helpless people. I didn't understand a thing. I was just happy that she was talking to me, willingly talking to me, not just small talk like "buy some milk." A real conversation . . .

I knew she didn't like him. And then that interview came out. Years after she won that beauty pageant, the newspapers were still interested in what Sigal Levin had to say. Usually she talked about jeans and a tan, but then that interview . . . and still, I didn't put it all together.

I wanted so badly for her to love me.

So, here goes, Ronit. I'm going to die. I have twenty-four hours, tops, because my assassin, Shimshon Krieker, has a plane ticket back to Israel. I never thought I'd live to see your divorce, and now I realize I won't live to see your wedding, either. Enjoy married life, dear sister. We were all right, weren't we? And your sweet fiancé is all right. Really, he's all right. You might, for transparency's sake, want to acknowledge the fact that he's a very successful banker who works for shady entities, handling complex money transfers to places all over the world. It isn't legal, and no one will ever catch him, so don't worry. It's the way these things are done. And most important, it's considered dignified in his homeland. He won't be taken down, and neither will you. You'll be a dignified, rich woman. Don't ask him too many questions. You don't want the armpits of his suits to stink. I miss Iris, you know?

I'm writing you this letter because my end is approaching. I don't object to Shimshon Krieker murdering me. I just want him to get caught and fried in the electric chair after I'm gone. So I'm sending this letter to you, along with everything necessary to incriminate this miserable assassin who's about to kill an HIV-positive guy with a chronic infection and deep depression. He told me he's flying back to Israel tomorrow, so it's probably going to happen tonight. He said he'd take me to the docks across from Randall's Island in the East River, because he has a surprise for me. I feel sorry for him. He must have thought his plan was foolproof, that he would stun the victim before I could even figure out what was happening. As God is my witness, I wasn't a bad man, no, and at the very least I think I deserve a better assassin. Maybe one who would actually like me. Shimshon Krieker is over seventy years old, muscular and dark, a little confused, a little crazy. The first time he wanted to show me how he swam in the Hudson at night I thought that was it, the murder was about to happen, but he actually took off his clothes under the bridge and went in for a swim. Amazing! Do you have any idea how cold the Hudson is at this time of year? Do you know what treacherous currents are moving beneath the oily shell of its New York waters? But there was that old man, swimming alone with the determination of a shark, waving to me. I just had to clap my hands. I was truly excited. Really. Then he took me out to a nice restaurant. There was a moment I thought he was actually interested in me, but no, I can read a situation quickly. He isn't interested in me, or in anyone else. By my assessment, he isn't even interested in sex, and never has been. He's interested in power. In force. Are you with me, Ronit? He told me he wanted to go to the Central Park Zoo, to see the lion. He said he had to. "I want to see if he can look me in the eyes," he said. Insane. We're dealing with a pathetic, insane murderer.

I'm so curious to know: Why? Why murder a half-dead guy who won't be around for very much longer, anyway? The curiosity is killing me, but if I ask him he'll know I get it, and things might go wrong. Then what? Go back to serving in the Army of Death, under the command of General Leg Infection? Go from a Mercedes to a Fiat? A scooter?

That's not why I'm writing to you, Ronit. I have to focus. I don't feel like writing a thirty-page letter you'll never even read because you can't be bothered with that kind of thing. I once wrote Cousin Julian a thirty-page letter. Just to set the record straight. I never heard back. Well, I'm veering off course again. Usually the focal point is the center of a circle, but there are many other mathematical forms that have a focal point, even two of them, and if you start thinking about Banach spaces, then . . . never mind. I'll focus in the simplest way possible, and get this done. I have a date with an assassin tonight.

The subject is Grandpa. Something I've discovered. Something that might explain things.

It all began with me deteriorating in every possible way. Physically, mentally, financially. The end. Here, in America, no money means no treatment, certainly not for someone in my condition. So they sent me to Nathan Smith, a charity institution where some good people treated me for free. They still are. One day last week a young, dedicated male nurse was changing my bandages when he realized I was from Israel and told me that there was an Israeli woman who worked there for years. She was considered the clinic's very own Mother Teresa. "She was superdevoted," this devoted man told me. He said that she was old now, retired, but she was still famous at the clinic, and because of her he considers all Israelis to be angels.

"Yes, that's true, we're all like that," I told him.

That sweet man, devoid of any sense of humor or irony, looked at me and said in perfect solemnity, "It's because you're from the Holy Land."

His eyes were so beautiful at that moment. So beautiful.

Then he said, "Her name was . . . something Indian."

"Indian?"

"Yes."

Listen, Ronit, I don't know where it came from, from some hard, dry, old, and completely locked place, but it suddenly shot out like a jet stream through all the layers, unbelievable, and I asked him, off the top of my head, "Sima?"

He got excited, hurting my leg a little in his enthusiasm. "Yes, Sima! You see? An Indian name!"

Ronit, Sima is the reason for this entire letter. From what abyss of irrationality and unreasonability and impossibility did that name emerge? If someone had pointed a gun to my head, back when that was still a threat to me, and demanded the name of the young nurse who used to work with Grandpa and disappeared one day, leading to all sorts of accusations against Grandpa, until she finally got in touch with her family from America, I wouldn't have been able to remember.

No chance.

How can I remember an anonymous, unimportant nurse who'd disappeared? A scandal that had been archived before I even turned three? When could my memory have absorbed any of this?

But it shot out: Sima.

Because there are things inside of us. Memories, thoughts, pain, emotion . . . locked as if inside a monster's fist. A fossilized fist that releases nothing, ever. They remain there, in the depths, bothering us our entire lives, without our even knowing, without being able to pull them out and deal with them.

Sima.

I'll make this short, Ronit, and get to the point of this fucking letter, which is taking all the strength I don't have. A letter from the night preceding certain death, in the style of the great French mathematician Évariste Galois, who left his entire mathematical vision in a stack of unreadable handwritten pages on the night before his death, delivered in a duel in which he sought to defend the honor of a questionable woman he didn't even know. Mathematicians used those pages to decipher problems that had been occupying their minds for years, an entire branch of modern math came out of the vision of this tortured young man, who was killed at nineteen. What a waste . . . what a waste. That's what everyone thinks about it today.

No one will think that about me.

I'm deviating again.

Oh well, a deviant. A crooked man. That's what I am.

I'm not leaving you a mathematical vision to make a fortune for mathematical minds. I'm leaving you something that might release a bothersome weight within you. Not even an uncracking of the truth, but something.

Long story short, I got in touch with that woman. To keep things aboveboard, I immediately introduced myself. The first thing she said, before I could even tell her what a wretched state I was in, was, "I didn't do anything. He made me do it until I finally ran away."

I was thinking of sexual abuse, rape, perversion. You know exactly what kind of man our renowned grandfather was.

I'm getting to the point, Ronit, I'm getting to the point. She wouldn't meet me. She threatened to call the cops. She's spent her whole life trying to heal from the pain, and wouldn't see anyone, talk to anyone, "most of all not his . . . grandson."

I'm getting there, Ronit, really, I am. I begged. I explained my situation. I didn't tell her an assassin was about to kill me, so she wouldn't think I was nuts. I used the faithful service of my leg infection again. I explained I was HIV positive, that . . . she got it. She felt sorry for me. She explained what to do when my condition worsened, who would treat me, even without money. She opened up a little. Not on the matter I was interested in, no, but I read things between the lines.

She talked in circles at first. Something about experiments, scientific vision, a hope for wondrous breakthroughs. I realized Grandpa had plucked her out of a nursing staff, turning her into a close, active partner for procedures that weren't in any protocol and were hidden from all. She admired him, was in love with him. He promised her he was just waiting for the right opportunity to leave his wife and marry her. You know, the usual . . . She cried. She cried for me, too. She wanted to hang up a few times. She *asked* to hang up but didn't just go ahead and do it. Maybe I was able to convince her I was one of the good guys, the . . . victims. Suddenly I told her how soon I was about to die. She was confused at that point, thought I was talking about suicide, begged me not to take that path, said I had a chance, I was still young, I had a future ahead of me. She agreed to tell me everything in return for my promise not to give up, not to choose that path. I promised.

It was one of the most profitable lies of my life.

If you can call what I heard *profitable*.

So, here goes, Ronit. Remember, when we were kids, that game in the newspaper? Connect the Dots? Remember how we fought over it, taking turns? (You always won.) So here, Ronit, grant me this special opportunity to connect the dots for you:

As far as I can understand, our grandfather, the great Dr. Levin, had his own private collection of scientific notions. He had ideas about assisting fertility, assisting women in endangered pregnancies. Problematic ideas. So he found patients who wouldn't complain, and he ran some experiments. That's what I've gathered. When the experiments didn't work out, he stopped. By the time he was appointed as hospital administrator, he didn't need those scientific discoveries anymore. He had enough reputation and glory, enough respect. The risk wasn't worth it. So he stopped. Anyone who complained was silenced. Everything was kept quiet, except for the conscience of the woman who worked closely with him, the young nurse Sima . . . She didn't say anything explicit, wouldn't give any details regarding what they did to whom and for how long and with what results. But you can figure it out, right? We had Dr. Mengele as a grandfather, Ronit. You get it?

We said good-bye in tears, mine and hers. A good woman. The last thing she said was, "I didn't do anything, and I'm going to burn in hell."

That's it, Ronit. I had to write it all down. So I could lament my life, so I could say good-bye to you, so that old bastard, Shimshon Krieker, can be indicted. I wrote this entire letter because I hope after you read it some heavy sadness in the bottom of your soul can finally be released, and you can live. We're all innocent, and all about to burn in hell. But I hope you won't.

I'm going to meet Shimshon Krieker now. I'll send this letter, along with the incriminating documents, on my way. I wish I could know what's going to happen, say, tomorrow morning. It's like putting a book down halfway through, dying without knowing how the story ends.

No matter.

Have a happy marriage, Ronit. You were a good sister. The best you could be. Kisses to you and your fiancé. Really. And watch out for bad people.

From your brother, who loves you in spite of being dead,

Keynan

CHAPTER 27

ZOE AND RAI IN A BLACK MERCEDES

"What is it, Zoe?"

"Your plans for the next two days? Cancel them."

"Oh yeah? Are you going to write my column for me and do construction work for me downtown?"

"Listen, I don't know if you've noticed what Mister Inspector Merlin did to us."

"Superintendent."

"What?"

"His rank is superintendent."

"He's pushed us aside, Rai. He used us and then threw us out like . . . Are you going to let him just walk all over us?"

"That isn't exactly—"

"Come on, I called us a cab. We're going to my father's house. You'll see your life finally taking off."

"I'm supposed to be a little scared, aren't I?"

Zoe giggled. She leaned in and kissed his forehead. "There's our cab."

The cab pulled up and they got in.

"To Ganei Yehuda, please, 4 HaEshel Street," Zoe instructed the driver.

Rai wanted to say something, to object, to protest, but Zoe fell asleep.

He watched her sleep.

She was wrong. Superintendent Merlin was like most cops. She was wrong, but he wished . . .

He just wanted a miracle, like in *Mary Poppins*, when a wind starts blowing and the long line of nannies waiting for their job interview gets blown away, and Mary Poppins lands in their place. He wanted a chilly wind to blow away the cop and the murder case and this entire city. He wanted for nothing to remain but him and this girl, Zoe Navon. He'd never felt that way before.

She must be a witch.

He watched her. A deep sleep. How quickly she fell into the deep sleep of babies. He always descended into sleep like a mole, digging the way in with his paws. *How did it come to her so easily?* When he was her age, he was already feeling complicated, guilty. Guilty for everything, without actually being guilty of anything.

Damn.

Rai slowly pulled some pages from his coat pocket. Serial killer or no, he had to submit his column on time. Meaning, he had to write it first. This time, the subject was "Everything is sheet," a message that recently had appeared in four different locations around the city. The letters were so precise and elegant. No stencil. A calligraphic craft, performed with extreme Japanese tenderness. So much effort and beauty were invested in the words. The effort was the message. He'd already written two hundred words just about that. He had two hundred more to go. A little more than that. He had to explain the desperate worldview expressed in the tools of a person who isn't prepared, or able, to act. A person giving in. Everything is *sheet*.

"No smoking in my cab."

Rai looked up. Zoe was to his right, awake, a slender cigarette in her dainty hand. She put the cigarette back in her purse.

"You're dust . . ." she mumbled hostilely at the driver.

The taxi turned at Savyon Junction, riding through the manicured streets of Ganei Yehuda.

"Stop here, please," Zoe told the driver.

"We're not at the address yet," the driver said.

"Stop. Thank you."

"There you go."

The taxi pulled up and Zoe paid the driver. Rai was afraid of this moment. He was the man; he was the wallet. *On the other hand . . .* But Zoe simply paid and got out, immediately lighting her cigarette.

"So you smoke?" he asked, jumping out after her.

"Not a lot, not a lot. But whenever I get to my dad's turf . . . I would have preferred something stronger. And booze. Lots of it. And an orgasm. An orgasm would have soothed me, but it isn't acceptable here in Ganei Yehuda."

"Daddy issues, huh?"

"I'll be fine."

"Are you the kind of family that doesn't speak? Rich people that hate each other? That kind of thing?"

"Rai Zitrin, you're growing some balls. But my father and I aren't the issue right now. He's been in the States for the past month. Come on, forget about family. We're on a mission."

"Mission? What kind of mission? What mission are we on?"

"We're going to stop a murderer."

Zoe threw her cigarette on a lawn. She walked past a small babbling fountain to a stylish metal gate and rang the bell. An Asian-accented voice asked over the intercom, "Miss Navon?" and an older Filipina woman stepped out of the house.

Rai looked at the name on the mailbox. "Victor Navon? Your father is Attorney Victor Navon?"

"Cool, huh? If they catch the serial killer alive, there's a chance my father will defend him, pro bono, just for fun. For the TV cameras."

"Your father is Attorney Victor Navon . . ."

"I call him Viper Navon—the evil half of my genes. My mother is the kind, helpless half that hurts the ones it loves."

"Wow, your father is Attorney Victor Navon . . ."

Zoe patted his back and said, "Something caught in your throat there?"

The Filipina woman opened the gate and apologized, adding, "The remote control is broken . . . ," while Rai gave in to the pat he could still feel on his back. He didn't normally like to be touched. Even during sex, touching . . . some part of him always wanted it, while another part pushed it away. Just like in winter, with the hot water in the shower—so good at first, then too hot. But this touch of hers felt good.

Witch.

Zoe went inside for a few minutes and then came out, waving fondly at the woman. "You've got a driver's license, right?" she asked Rai. A steel garage door slowly lifted and Rai found himself looking with alarm at a shiny black Mercedes, the kind that wasn't meant to move from display rooms to real roads.

He drove. Without much confidence.

"You've got to get us down to the desert as fast as you can. To Kidra. So start showing signs of control over my father's monster."

"All right, all right. I haven't driven in I don't know how long . . . and this thing . . . there're too many buttons. Say, I realize this isn't really a subject we want to go into, but your father has no idea we're using his car, does he?"

"We're on a holy mission, just like the Blues Brothers."

"I'm also not sure about the . . . I haven't been outside of Tel Aviv in forever. I worked in the Hadera forest for a few days three months ago . . ."

"The desert will refresh you."

"How do I get there? And where the hell is Kidra?"

"Right by the Kidra Stream, obviously. A deep canyon burrowing into marlstone cliffs and chalk rocks. It is famous for the floods that happen there from time to time, attracting tourists and adventurers. Google it."

"Did Google tell you how to get there?"

A truck passed them, sounding a long honk. *A warning? A threat? A tease? Rage? Admiration for the shiny black car?* The language of honking wasn't one of subtleties.

"Don't worry, this car has GPS. I'll turn it on, and you just listen to the directions. Now, think carefully, Rai Zitrin, do you prefer a male or female voice?"

"What?"

"You can get directions from the GPS in a male voice, if that's what you like, getting ordered around by a man, or in a female voice, if you prefer that. We don't have the voice of someone with an ambiguous sexual identity. Sorry."

Rai looked at her silently.

"Your face looks like it's 'recalculating.' I'm going to pick a female voice for you. I believe in you, Rai Zitrin. Let's go to the desert."

She entered some information and then leaned back in her seat, content. A soft female voice gave Rai the first instruction.

Rai gripped the steering wheel with two fists. What was he doing? He had to demand an explanation. What were they going to do when they got there? What did she think they were capable of? He turned to confront Zoe, but she was already asleep.

"In five hundred meters, turn left," said the soft female voice.

With no other choice, Rai Zitrin steered Attorney Victor Navon's car southward to the desert through a sealed-off, air-conditioned silence, nothing shifting or twitching, other than his clenched hands, which gripped the wheel, and the sporadic instructions of the GPS.

When Zoe woke up and sluggishly rubbed her eyes, he pounced.

"So what exactly is your plan? Because we're getting closer and . . . and I have no idea what you're going to do."

She silently looked at him for a moment, placing him in her world as she ascended from the depths of her dream.

"We're going to find this place, some sort of secluded settlement outside of Kidra. There's an office there. I've already spoken to Sarit, the secretary. We're going there to protect Gili Levin."

"Until the police arrive. Once they arrive, we're definitely unnecessary."

"Cops are 'dust' at best, and right now Superintendent Jonah Merlin is 'please destroy,' as far as I'm concerned. That nag. We can't trust them to stop the killer from reaching Gili Levin, even if they surround her with spears in their hands."

"I'm guessing we can't stop, right? Bathroom? Coffee break?"

"We're not stopping. Look, Maria gave me some sandwiches and spicy Philippine salad. You can take a bathroom break, if the alternative is leaving a puddle on my dad's car seat."

"Got it. I can hold it in for now."

Zoe gave him a long, dark, inscrutable look. She sighed, turned on a small reading light, and pulled the white Bruno Schulz book from her bag.

"Why did he have to latch on to Bruno, that murderer? Couldn't he have used Kurt Cobain quotes? Or something by Louis-Ferdinand Céline? Why Bruno?"

"Can I tell you something?"

"What?"

"I read a lot. Good books, not trash, and I swear, I swear, I've never heard of Bruno Schulz."

"Oh, of course, because I made him up, right?"

"Enough. This aggression is unnecessary. In general, as long as I'm the one with a driver's license around here, why don't you try being nice?"

"Your suggestion has been noted. Speaking of a driver's license, I brought something else, just in case. Do you have a license for this?" Zoe said, as her delicate hand fished a glinting black gun from her purse.

The car swerved, then straightened out.

"Are you nuts?"

"You're nuts. We're driving toward a murderer. Murderers."

"But where . . ."

"Oh, it was nothing. Attorney Victor Navon has to keep a few guns under his pillow, to make it all soft and—"

"We're not going to use that."

"We're not excited about the prospect, I agree. But for right now, this gun is loaded."

"Are you serious? I'm pulling over."

"Oh, relax. The safety is on. I'm serious. What, you're not turned on by a girl with a gun?"

"I'm turned on by the idea of not being here, you know? I can't believe this . . . Where is my life? I'm driving Attorney Victor Navon's car without his knowledge or permission, and now I have his gun . . . without a license . . . Is this for real?"

"And you're on your way to meet a murderer. You forgot to freak out about that. Rai Zitrin, let's get some action in our lives, why don't we?"

He said nothing. A thick silence. What was he doing?

"Or emotion . . . let's get some emotion in our lives," Zoe said in a quiet, whiny voice, a pleasant voice.

Witch.

"Do you really know Polish?"

"Yes. Not fluently, but yes."

"And it's only . . ."

"So I could read him. And some good poets. If Carmela Tzedek only knew that poetry was Zoe Navon's destiny."

"How did you even hear about this writer? What's so great about him?"

"The librarian at the city library gave me his books. There was a period when I went there every day. While my mother thought I was sleeping around with older men and doing hard drugs, I'd be sitting in the library reading, along with all the ugly ducklings who spend their days there. I had to breathe the air they exhaled."

"And you fell in love with him?"

"Not right away. He really is a handful at first. But this nice older man noticed me reading him and started chatting with me. He seemed like big-time 'dust' at first, but I slowly realized he was something else. He didn't stare at my chest like you do, and he helped me discover Bruno Schulz. Since then, this book has been my bible. Actually, more like one scroll. Because Bruno published his first story collection in 1934 and the second in 1937, and while he was working on his big novel, *The Messiah*, World War II broke out. The novel was gone, lost in oblivion, and Bruno Schulz was shot in the street. November 19, 1942, to be exact. Did I tell you what people say, about how he died?"

"You haven't really spoken to me before. You've mostly insulted me."

"You need a glass for those tears?"

The GPS cut in and told them to turn left. Zoe looked at the map on the screen.

"We're not far. Listen, this is a story that may not be true. Or maybe it is. They say the Nazi who kept Bruno Schulz alive in exchange for Bruno sorting the art he'd pillaged was on bad terms with another Nazi. When, one day, he killed that other Nazi's Jewish protégé, he went over to tease his adversary, telling him what he'd done. According to the story, the other Nazi told him something like, 'You've killed my Jew? Very well. Now I will kill your Jew.' And that's it. He went off and found poor Bruno on the street. November 19, 1942."

"Is that a true story? It's horrifying."

"The Holocaust was pretty horrifying, Rai. But forget it, I don't want to insult you now. Listen, one time I went to hear a lecture by this author who said that was the very essence of the Nazi attitude, the idea that people were interchangeable. Your Jew, my Jew. The very opposition of the humane attitude, which sees each person as unique, a world of his or her own, irreplaceable. It was so beautiful, the way he said it . . . so true."

"You know what? On the one hand, you said an entire nice sentence without insulting anybody. On the other hand, you aren't a strong proponent of that attitude he was talking about. Calling people 'dust' and 'nobodies' isn't really—"

"Forget about me now. I'm not perfect. I'm Attorney Victor Navon's daughter. Think about Bruno Schulz. The victim. That poor man, who didn't even stand a chance. It happens to me every time—I feel sorry for this man who was murdered fifty years before I was born, and then I start feeling sorry for myself. You know, Rai, how many times I cried—sobbed, with my entire body—because I started by thinking about Bruno and finished by thinking about myself?"

He glanced at her. Tears were in her eyes. She looked at him, touched her finger to her eye and put it to his lips.

"Here, have a taste."

He did.

"Oh, Mom, if you'd only started taking lovers a little earlier, I might have been the daughter of a nice man."

The highway was behind them. They drove through narrow, twisty side roads strewn with pebbles.

"I can't believe I'm driving your father's car without his knowledge."

Zoe glanced at him for a moment. Cold, detached. For the past twenty minutes she'd been flipping through Bruno Schulz's book; the reason for their excursion seemed to have left her mind, and most of all the man driving her father's car, who was sporadically burning up with alarm.

He looked straight ahead. If she wanted to disconnect, let her disconnect.

"Hey, Rai, are you focused?"

Their eyes met.

"I'm completely focused. I'm going to put this car back in its garage without a scratch. Without a scratch, you hear me?"

"Don't worry. My dad's taken quite a bit of crap from me over the years, and he deserves every little bit. He knows. You remember Solomon, that crazy homeless man who walked around King Solomon Street for years? I was very impressed by his poetic choice to wander that specific street, and I paid him an existence stipend for a while, out of the cash my father had in his safe."

"Are you serious?"

"So, at some point, my father stopped getting paid in cash. I did a good thing, didn't I?"

"And he had no idea it was you? He never found out?"

"I don't know; we never discussed it."

The GPS cut in again, instructing them in her pleasant voice.

"We're close," said Rai. "You think this is a race against time? Do you have any idea?"

"No idea. But that Jonah Merlin is going to get his. Him and Carmela Tzedek."

"I want coffee, and there's no chance of that happening. I need to pee. There's still a chance of that. I want time to pass already. I'm dying for time to pass."

"The funny thing is that we even feel desires regarding time," Zoe said sleepily. "We want it to move fast; we want it to move slowly. What good is it? Has anyone ever been able to affect time? When . . ."

She fell asleep on his shoulder, right as they were about to get there. They were so close.

The female voice of the GPS said, "In five hundred meters, turn left." And then, a moment later, "You have reached your destination."

CHAPTER 28

ELIYAHU SELFTER—NOT TO BE ALONE FOR A BIT

We're on our way, Ephraim. Just a little longer, one big finale. Then we can rest. But before we rest, I promised you a big trip in the Land of Israel. Here, we're on our way. That good man, Shimshon Krieker, will take us to a place where I'll show you what to do. Then we rest. It's good you don't read the papers, Ephraim. People are writing awful things. Maybe it was my mistake, not explaining what I was doing. But it doesn't matter. Because our justice isn't for those living here, in this world. It's for the one looking down at us from the heavens, Ephraim. The one looking down and thanking us.

My mother cried once, Ephraim. She told me, "You can be a writer, you have all the right traits." I'm a little embarrassed to tell you this, but in my entire life, I've barely read a book. That's why, when I found a book wrapped in fabric underneath all of Barney Landman's guns and rifles and semiautomatics, I thought it had something to do with his evil business. Either that, or a rifle maintenance guide. I put it in the new hiding place without opening it and then forgot all about it. The book just lay there, for years.

For fifty years.

When I began preparing this operation, when I went over there to get my weapons out of the hiding place, my fingers were drawn to it. I finally looked at the book, and what did I find in that evil villain's stash? You won't believe it, Ephraim. I found a thin book by Bruno Schulz . . . in Polish . . . a first edition, from the time it was first published in Poland, the land of evil. How did a book like that make it into Barney Landman's things? Different passages were marked in the book. Someone marked down important sentences. Who did that? At that moment, I felt my father, from his death in the dark hole of Warsaw, greeting me, saying, "Go, go, Eliyahu, go, go forth and prosper. You must take your revenge for everything that's been done to you, and let me participate. I'm dead, hunched down in a hole, just like in your dreams, just like in the books you used to flip through in the old library at school, the books that were only laid out on the table on Holocaust Remembrance Day, and even though I'm dead, let me be a part of it. Take these quotes from Bruno Schulz's book, write them down wherever you act so that the whole world can know you're taking revenge not only for what they did to Rachel, your wife, Ephraim's mother, but so that all victims will be silent no longer. And I know, Eliyahu, my son, that you've filed a complaint about Dr. Levin, damn his name, at the Ministry of Health, at the police, that you've spoken to lawyers, to the Doctors Union. Eliyahu, my son, you tried to avoid violence, but they left you no choice. I'll be with you, Eliyahu. We'll all be together."

You know, Ephraim, that's what my father told me when I held the first edition of the book written by his soul mate, Bruno Schulz. And if, for years before that, I'd planned my operation, never knowing for sure if it would work, I suddenly realized that something this great, something that goes back to the days of Cain and Abel, of the Bible, could never fail. I realized that my father would take my revenge with me, that the great Bruno Schulz would take my revenge through me, that you, Ephraim, that I didn't get a special boy like you by chance. You are the hammer that all the victims hold, together, and each time you—with your hands—do justice, all the victims in their graves will be with us. That's how I felt. That I wouldn't be alone.

Forgive me, Ephraim, for what I'm about to say. I'm asking for your forgiveness, my good boy, for feeling good about it, because I've felt alone for so many years, so many years—only you and I, so alone.

CHAPTER 29

GILI LEVIN

I taught myself not to want my own child, and suddenly . . .

It was a long course, and there were many moments where I was tempted to drop out. A child . . . But I completed the course and told myself, *Ask yourself and listen to the answer.* So I asked, and I answered: *No.* Finally, *no.* Loud and clear. No fluttering tail of a wish not yet surrendering, no longer able to articulate itself with words, but still with a remainder of a body, a spore, a sperm. Oh, those images . . . but I finally asked myself and answered: *No.*

I've always wanted it to end, this thing I can't name, this thing I've been fighting against my entire life, this thing in our family. To end, even if I had no idea what it was. No children. That was the solution.

I've always carefully looked both ways. My brother, Julian? No kids. Not even close. If there's one thing he's always held sacred, it's condoms. The beautiful, ambitious, frivolous Ronit—no kids. She was the classic candidate for the role of the exhausted, divorced mother of two. And Iris, the only one who was ever worthy, so noble, died without leaving a trace of her existence in this world. In her last days, I was at her bedside, stroking her hair. The one and only. The one and only who was worthy. Keynan, my eldest cousin, well, with him nothing is unequivocal. He once told me about an attempt he'd made, something . . . long story short, the girl told him she was pregnant, then disappeared. Of all people, Keynan, the one time he slept with a woman, he became a father. Probably. He never dared find out for sure, not that he even cared. My cousins on Mom's side, Sybil and Bernard and Luciana, they're full of life and children. Wild Belgians of all ages, calling me "Auntie" with the accent of coal miners, making me happy. The problem is on my father's side. I would have guessed it was with my father, but Keynan, Ronit, Iris—the problem is higher up the generational ladder. It had to end.

Then suddenly I met this savage, this rude man in uniform, and I showed him what's what. We fought like two male ibexes on a slope. Eventually I pulled him down to my hard tatami mat, and I just know I got pregnant. Well, for once in my life, I also deserve to be a mindless bimbo from a nice neighborhood. Sixth floor with a view of something. A gym membership. Attempting to grow herbs on the windowsill.

What I'm trying to say is, he's married.

I took a married man inside of me and I got pregnant. I'm sure of it. I know how to listen to my body. My body is pregnant. I've felt it making thousands of little adjustments to the new situation since yesterday: the tiny stretching, the balance of energy between organs. I'm pregnant. And he's married. And he's an idiot. A superintendent in the Israel Police.

Why couldn't I have just fallen for a butcher?

But I'm planning on carrying the child of Superintendent Dido Partuk, that sweet little goat, in my womb for nine months, and then give birth to it.

I've decided.

Superintendent Dido Partuk: the moment he called the office and spoke to Sarit, she had him pegged. She told me it was some baboon who thought I needed protection. I had no idea the entire country was panicking over some elusive murderer. I was at workshops, then took a group to see a Flood Vision. Then he gets here, with his police cruiser, like some beast, very confident, giving me that look, the look I know so well, his mind probably forming his opinion of me: "She's pretty but so bland. And no boobs." I know how it goes. He starts preaching to me about the complexity of the situation.

First he makes sure I'm not the murderer, and I happily give him the entire desert as my alibi. Then he starts explaining that I might be next. The next victim. Maybe. Unclear. So, just in case, he has to watch out for me. I feel my body beginning to gather energy so that I can properly deal with this elephant that wants to bring his filth into my clean circle.

Then he tells me that Ronit has been murdered. That Julian has been murdered. That Keynan is missing.

I dim certain parts and illuminate others. I deal. I feel things cracking. Hear the sounds of rocks falling. I don't have the power to gather myself. I don't have the power to gather myself. *Julian? Does Dad know?*

And he asks me, "Would you like some tea? Anything else? Maybe you should sit down."

He's transparent before me, and his eyes are still sizing up my stalk-like body. Sorry that I'm so bland.

Superintendent Dido Partuk didn't change during his few days in the desert. He searched for cell service like a dog sniffing for the scents of other dogs, his self-confidence overflowing like sewage. Such uncrackable strength. The sealed rock of his mind.

A day and a half later, he goes away for a few hours, leaving another officer in his place. Dumb, but quiet. Then he returns, bringing back an electric razor, a toaster, a microwave, two chargers for his Motorola, a portable DVD player, and an MP3 player. He connects all the appliances and begins dirtying up the air with rattles and beeps and hums.

In the meantime, I'm collapsing. Standing barefoot, two feet on the ground, erect, and falling into an abyss. Julian. *Why Julian? And why Ronit?* And Keynan. *What do they know about Keynan?*

Dido Partuk doesn't know. He promises to find out. My air is filled with the sounds of his appliances.

Why Julian?

I weaken.

Then a shiny baby-blue car arrives. These aren't my tourists coming to see the Flood Vision. They would come thirty minutes later. It's a woman, for him. He made an appointment. A woman in a white skirt, a red tank top, and flip-flops, the kind that pretend to be shabby but are very expensive, studded. She comes out of the car. They kiss.

He turns to Sarit. Not to me. He asks her if there's a place nearby with no people around.

I tell him his date is canceled.

At night he comes out with me, a security force of one stupid man. My tourists are a group of five guys from Afula who decided that watching a flood at Kidra Stream would be part of a bachelor party. I expected the worst, but they turn out to be real princes, quiet and kind, curious and cooperative.

And the biggest surprise? Superintendent Dido Partuk doesn't accompany us with the ruckus of a hippopotamus but instead slips alongside, stealthily, smoothly. Most of the time we can't even see him. Only the smell of his oiled gun invades my nostrils, alerting me to his presence.

The flood begins at 3:00 a.m., ahead of schedule, but we still manage to welcome it, sitting on the huge flat rock that hangs above the ravine, watching the water rushing with a Genghis Khan might. I need to calculate when the ravine would look completely dry again, so that the next flood would be impressive, and I already have a tour booked, a man in a wheelchair with two escorts. But my mind, my soul, my body—they all continue to collapse into the dark elements of energy, into the moment of creation. *How could it be? My brother . . . my cousins . . . murdered?*

Get a grip. Follow the meridians. Clarity. I console myself that I would soon return to the rock, to the stream, with the next customers. One of the clients has already been down here two and a half weeks ago. Shimshon Krieker. He signed up for a Flood Vision but wasn't disappointed when the flood didn't come. I apologized. It ended up not raining in the mountains. He kissed my hand like some kind of Russian nobleman and promised to come back. The whole time I thought about how strange he was. How he was a little . . . like me. Without a flood to look at, we spent the entire night sitting on that rock and talking. In the morning, he told me how happy he was to know me.

Around noon, as I say good-bye to the five young guys, and just so I don't accidentally start thinking that the male race has changed, they confess they're headed to Eilat, where a stripper and a casino boat are waiting for them. I turn around after they leave, headed for my clean circle, and Superintendent Dido Partuk stands there, meaning that there is no cleanliness and no chance of being alone. My guardian, my defender, this idiot whose chest hair shows through every piece of clothing he wears. Suddenly I'm filling up with my inner substance, my body sounds a mighty cry, and with no other choice I take him by the hand over to my tatami mat. If he gets to fuck me, at least let it be hard on his back.

CHAPTER 30

BEFORE THE FLOOD

The first malfunction occurred in his conversation with Sarit Katznelson, Gili Levin's personal assistant. Up until that moment, Jonah Merlin gave dozens of orders and made sure to summon police officers from the Aravot Station, the civilian rescue unit, even a military helicopter team. Before him he saw cops running around, handing him files to sign, passing him notes. Commander Menashe Bried also appeared to tell him something. Everything progressed at a dizzying pace, a kind of race against time for the sake of rescuing one woman, somewhere in the heart of the desert.

Then came the conversation with Sarit Katznelson.

Superintendent Merlin dialed the number.

A cheerful, positive voice answered, "Hello, this is Kidra Travel. If the call disconnects, I'll call you back within a minute."

"Hello, is this Gili Levin?"

"No, this is her assistant, Sarit Katznelson. Are you interested in—"

"Sarit, I have to speak to Gili."

"That's impossible. She's on her way to a Flood Vision with her clients."

"Sarit, this is Superintendent Jonah Merlin. This is a matter of life and death for Gili. You—"

The call disconnected.

As promised, within seconds Sarit was on the line again, in full-on friendly mode.

"I'm back, sir. I apologize, our cell reception is faulty to the point of almost being nonexistent, but that's what's so wonderful about this place."

He breathed heavily.

"This is Superintendent Jonah Merlin. Gili Levin's life is in immediate, real danger. Do you have any customers that answer the following description: a man in a wheelchair and a giant escort? And possibly a third man? They're murderers. They want to kill Gili. Either put her on or warn her for me or—"

Disconnected.

A minute later, Sarit is on the phone again.

Merlin shouted, "Where's Superintendent Dido Partuk? Is he with her?"

"Listen to me, sir. Gili Levin isn't stupid. She knows exactly who those people she's with are. I know, too. We both know."

"And?"

"You don't know Gili Levin. She has her own ways."

"Are you crazy? Are you completely insane?"

"I'm not insane. I'm Sarit Katznelson."

"What?"

"I'm a descendant of the author Yehuda Leib Katznelson, better known by his pen name, Buki Ben Yogli."

Breathe. Regroup. Superintendent Merlin tried again.

"Sarit, please. Where's Superintendent Partuk?"

"He's with them. Gili convinced him that it was all for the best. He's guarding her. I guess. Believe me, she's the one protecting all of us. And it's all for the best."

"Oh God! Is there anyone else there I can talk to?"

Disconnected.

This time Sarit didn't call him back.

Merlin's heart was racing.

Shulamit Tal informed him that Dido wasn't answering his phone, but it might just be a reception issue down in the Kidra Stream ravine. The rescue unit people called to say they were familiar with the terrain, including the area with no cell service, and that they were on their way. Same with the military rescue unit and the local police.

"So am I," said Merlin. "I'm heading down there."

He regretted not filling the gas tank last night.

Merlin made sure to dial all the numbers he could think of. He tried to get in touch with Vadim Kelsitz, with Dido, with anyone. The Aravot Station said that their police officers were almost there. He raced down the shoulder of the road alongside heavy traffic, headed south until Rishon L'Zion, where he finally merged into the lighter traffic at a mad speed. The gas level indicator lit up after he passed Gedera. He ignored it. *Whatever happens, happens. Just go.* He passed Kiryat Gat. Two more hours and he'd be there.

A sound of surrender rose from the belly of the car. A terrible crackle. Three indicators lit up. A revolting burnt smell of . . . What was that? He pulled over. Thick smoke poured from the hood.

As if it had been waiting in the dark, the rain began just as Merlin got out of his car and ran to the gas station in the distance. Kelsitz called, informing him of his meeting with Sarit Katznelson. His assessment was that the woman was crazy.

"I know," Merlin replied. "Get the route of the tour out of her. Think of something. She might have a map file in her office. Go crazy. Go privately. Do what you've got to do."

He was panting. His lungs wheezed. During his discounted trial membership at the Defense Force gym, he had focused on trying out the Italian espresso and the healthy sandwiches at the gym cafeteria.

The whole thing seemed too expensive. Hadas had enrolled and insisted that he enroll, too. The trial ended with a temporary verdict of "maybe." Now his lungs got the best of him. His knees hurt, too. Where was he running to, anyway?

At the gas station, a bespectacled guy with an elegant sport jacket and a fashionable overcoat had just finished filling up a new Audi and was sliding back into his car. Under the roof of the station, the rain stopped pounding down on Merlin, who startled the guy when he stood before him, sweating, dripping, panting.

"Please, give me the car. I'm a police officer. This is an emergency."

The driver was alarmed. And skeptical.

Superintendent Merlin pulled out his badge.

"I don't want to," the guy said and tried to shut the car door, but Merlin grabbed it.

"I . . . order . . . you," Merlin said, hyperventilating, pulling a business card from his pocket. "Call this number . . . tomorrow . . . and you'll get the car back."

The phone in Merlin's pocket began ringing.

The driver looked at him.

Merlin pulled out his gun and demanded, "Get out of the car. This is an emergency."

The driver got out carefully. A gas station attendant in uniform and a few other onlookers moved closer. Someone called the police.

"I'm a lawyer," said the driver. "The Special Investigations Unit will be all over you."

"Emergency," Merlin said, steadying his breath.

"Emergency, my ass," said the driver. "You're going to hear from me."

"He's right!" someone shouted from the dark. "Police state!"

Merlin sat down in the car. He glanced at the dashboard and asked the driver, "What's the key code?"

The driver walked away, pretending not to hear.

Merlin jumped out of his seat and yelled, "What's the key code?"

The driver ran into the gas station's little café, pulled a phone from his pocket, and dialed. Other drivers cut their refueling process short and drove away. The station attendant remained nearby.

"All I have is a moped," he said, his voice trembling.

Merlin decided to call the station and ask for a replacement car. Not that it would do any good. He wouldn't be arriving anywhere on time.

His phone rang again. Kelsitz. Sarit was going to take them to the flood lookout point. "And Merlin, your girl, Zoe, she's here. With her guy. She was the one who got the assistant to cut the bullshit. Blat."

It began raining harder. Across the street, in a small shopping center, he spotted a sign gleaming through the raindrops: "JACK BAGELS OPEN 24 HOURS."

Jack Bagels! He happened to have some coupons . . .

A little luck. Maybe just a little luck. He tossed the keys to the Audi on the driver's seat and began trudging through the rain toward the sign.

CHAPTER 31

FLOOD

Can you hear yourself, Zoe Navon? First of all, think of how it all ended well, how from the very first moment things worked out. Then think about what keeps racing in front of your eyes: people killing each other, yelling, gunshots, blood. Think of how it all ended well. *Try.*

But it won't let go, huh? Just you wait and see what's going to happen in your dreams tonight, Zoe Navon.

It really did seem at first that you were the queen of all crime scenes. You even thought that maybe you should have let poor Rai take a bathroom break, have some coffee, because you were almost *too* ahead of schedule. If you'd been just a little hastier, everything might have turned around in a bad way. Fifteen minutes before Dad's Mercedes, one of Merlin's cops arrived at the Kidra Travel office, a biker named Vadim Kelsitz, and by the time the Mercedes pulled up, he'd managed to get into a fight with Gili Levin's assistant with no positive results. If you'd been a little earlier, Zoe, you would have been the one fighting with her.

Even before Kelsitz got there, three cops from the Aravot Station showed up. Merlin had summoned them, too. They also paced the office, helpless, because just like Kelsitz, they were met by the strictest blockade in the universe: an old single woman with a well-formed life view. You'll be one of those one day, but a little different.

Not that you're clear on everything that happened before you got there, but just as Rai was maneuvering the car in front of the mud hut that serves as an office for these two nutjobs, Kelsitz walked out and tried to speak to Merlin on the phone. *Speak?* Carmela Tzedek would have demanded, and rightfully so, that you find a more fitting word. He yelled. He screamed. He roared. In short, he sent the insects flying with his screeches.

It was a classic moment for a girl like you, Zoe. It was time to get into the "Zoe, who's here to help" character. Kelsitz and the local cops were walking around in circles, trying to figure out a way to crack Gili's assistant's steel head as she sat in the office, refusing to reveal Gili's whereabouts and the route of the tour, though she clearly realized that the murderer was there with her.

Oh, Zoe. You must have been glowing with that role even before you walked inside, because the cops immediately surrounded you, trying to get a sympathetic gesture out of you. They were stuck with someone who was completely at peace, who informed them that Gili certainly did know she was touring the desert with someone who'd come down especially to kill her.

Kelsitz asked, "Is she armed?"

One of the cops, mimicking Sarit, quoted her in all seriousness, "Of course not! Gili Levin has her own ways."

At that moment you ordered the cops, "Wait here, and don't cause any trouble. I'll be back in a minute with the object's precise location."

"The object." Well, with a gun in your jacket pocket you felt entitled to use the term.

Then you walked into that office mud pile and found, besides a few phones and one fax machine, Miss Assistant Sarit Katznelson. Not sitting on a chair but rather on a white mat in the center of an almost empty room. Just like that. At the center of all this white was a lady that should have been married with kids, wearing white, with white exposed thighs, giving you a smile that melts orphans' deepest traumas, not realizing that those kinds of smiles turn Zoe Navon into a toxic hedgehog.

But you had a role to play. You lied to her softly, saying, "My uncle, he wants to murder Gili Levin. I came to talk him out of it. I'm his favorite niece. He'll listen to me. He isn't a bad person, truly he isn't. He's searching for a way to stop himself, and I can lead him there. He doesn't really want to hurt anyone."

She rose from the mat—you would have expected a more graceful motion from a woman who spends her entire life in yoga postures—and looked at the ceiling with an expression like "Thank you, spirits of the heavens, for granting me this blessed benevolence," and then said, "Her paths are peaceful. Come, I'll take you to them."

Her paths are peaceful? You had a dilemma, because the safety of the gun in your coat pocket was on, and perhaps this was your moment to switch it off. You'd never shot anything but a street sign. A serial killer was a bit more responsive.

You thought she'd run with you, and that it would take all the hours that a lady with such developed thighs needed to cover distances, but Sarit slipped into a mud hut next to the mud office and emerged on a red ATV, and you started pumping her brain with excuses about why Kelsitz and Rai *had* to come with you. You left the Aravot cops behind. They're big boys; they'd figure out something.

The moment you headed out, Sarit was reincarnated into the late Formula One race car driver Ayrton Senna, and with every sharp turn on the edge of the abyss, Kelsitz's face grew more pale, and Rai clung to you as if, by the laws of physics, something as tiny as Zoe Navon could really help his stability. Sarit focused on driving, and you focused on the fact that you actually had no idea what you were heading toward and what you just wasted hours of driving on. Suddenly it really wasn't clear. Carmela Tzedek would have liked the next metaphor for your growing turmoil, Zoe: You slowly realized that besides the roar of the engine, another wild sound was growing in the distance. A violent sound. The flood. But before you realized this, you asked yourself, *Is it my heart? My nerves? My fear? Mommy . . .*

As God as your witness, each year you used a different technique to avoid school field trips. In ninth grade you puked your guts out in the principal's office to convince her that you were unsuitable for journeys beyond the home, and so, when you heard the sound, forces of nature and creation weren't your first or second guess. You never believed something like this could exist, such a crushing sound, as if every student in every classroom was dragging their desk and seat all at once. But after one more bend in the road, when Sarit tilted her entire body to keep the ATV in the narrow lane, you were suddenly exposed to the full vision. An evil, full yellow moon and a ravine in which bursting waters roared and screamed, like a million streams thrown together, pouring over each other. Everything was shiny, everything was noisy, everything else was unimportant, because right in front of you, a large rock hung over the ravine, and on top of it was the entire group for which you'd just made this journey, exactly as they'd been described to you.

Almost exactly.

The disabled man wasn't in his wheelchair but instead was being carried by the giant. Well, there wasn't really much time to take in the size of the giant, because your appearance, and especially Kelsitz's appearance, jumping off the moving vehicle, led to an immediate, violent chain of events.

Right before your eyes, second by second . . .

The disabled man pulls out a big black gun from under his blanket and shoots the cop escorting Gili Levin—one bullet in the chest. The cop falls down. You'll later find out he died. Later you'll see the other cops from his station, grown men, sitting huddled together outside the Kidra Travel office and crying. *Really. Crying.*

A moment after the gunshot, Kelsitz charges the group and fires his gun. You think the giant is hit, maybe even twice, because the paralyzed man is dropped from his arms and lands on the rock in a strange position, his legs stretched out before him, like a kid in a bathtub. You realize he took a bullet, too, but he's shouting something at the giant, and the next thing you know the giant has his arms around Kelsitz, crushing him. This giant is a veritable mountain. You watch, pinned in place like a popsicle stick, as Rai jumps on the giant, on his neck, using all the muscles he's spent his life developing, and then you see the paralyzed guy picking up his gun again, as if remembering its existence, and aiming it at Gili Levin, who stands still a few meters away, without any intention of getting involved in this commotion. She looks at the dead cop, and there's something else there, in her eyes. These are things Zoe notices even in her most hysterical moments.

Suddenly a chopper appears above. You can't hear it because of the thunder of the flood, and it must be unable to land in the narrow ravine, because ropes come down and people loaded with equipment slide down them. The chopper's light beam reveals a vision Carmela Tzedek could have discussed for hours. Five men fighting each other like crazy, and three women standing and watching them from three different corners.

What does *that* say about the role of the woman in the modern age? Go to hell, Carmela Tzedek.

In the meantime, Gili Levin is standing, peaceful, staring at the paralyzed man about to shoot her. You see Sarit "Her-paths-are-peaceful" Katznelson gaping, perhaps still waiting for you, Zoe, to address your uncle. Peace to her peaceful paths. And you? You're only seventeen years old, and this kind of place is not for you. You can't move your body, can't even move your thoughts. You just see it all, every little detail, with deranged sharpness.

Rai is amazing. He manages to release Kelsitz from the giant's grip, and Kelsitz rolls back like Bruce Willis and shoots. Well, Bruce Willis would have hit the target. Kelsitz misses. At the same moment, the old man shoots. A flash of fire bursts out of his gun, but that's it. The people in the chopper might be shooting, too. Lots of explosions, but nobody falls down. Suddenly—maybe the shots wake up your brain—you recall that there's supposed to be another man in the murder party. You've listened carefully to all the cops' conversations; you remember. Your brain begins to wake up, asking where the third one is, as if there aren't enough killers on the scene already, and this thing happens, this image, that hasn't left you since. The old man shouts something—you can't hear him—and the giant takes him in his arms. They're both red with blood in the moonlight. As they step off the rock and into the ravine, falling into the flood, a creature emerges from below, from within the terrible water, a man-shaped thing, and snatches Gili Levin in his arms, and before anyone can move, both pairs are in the raging water.

You run ahead, and Sarit beats you there, and in the water you see this human creature, the third murderer, who you later realize is named Shimshon Krieker, trying to drown Gili Levin, his chin on her head, pushing her under the water.

The people in the chopper aim their weapons at Shimshon Krieker, whose body seems to be in control of the situation, in spite of the powerful currents.

Then two bullets leave your father's gun. Bam, bam. And Shimshon Krieker must be hit, because he lets go of Gili Levin, and all at once she spins in an eddy and gets caught between two rocks in the ravine and hangs on to one of them. Shimshon doesn't give up, but Kelsitz points his gun at him and shoots and shoots and shoots and hits and hits and hits.

And I'm only seventeen years old and I start crying.

It took us forever to get back to the Kidra Travel office, which suddenly looks like the sweet home I've never had. They wrapped a blanket around me, I don't know why. People watch survivors in movies and that's the rule—the guys in the rough gray blankets are those that had just been through hell.

I was supposed to sit there, wrapped in my blanket, and realize I'd killed a man. *But no.* Technically, what drove away those thoughts altogether was Officer Kelsitz, who even at the scene, seconds after Shimshon Krieker dropped dead into the flood, yelled like mad, "The last bullet was mine! The last bullet calls it! Cause of death: Vadim!" By the time we got back to Kidra Travel, we heard him repeat it again and again to anyone who would listen: "The last bullet calls it! Cause of death: Vadim!"

With the blanket around my shoulders, I heard him call Superintendent Merlin and repeat his pronouncements proudly, then curse, "It got disconnected. Blat."

He never even found the time to thank wonderful Rai, who saved him from the giant's claws. There was no sign of the giant and the disabled man; their bodies would only be found a full day later, way down in the ravine. Rai stroked my hair and rubbed my shoulder. Maybe ugly gray blankets turn him on.

Kelsitz paused in front of us and, instead of saying thank you, announced, "Last bullet was mine. Last bullet calls it."

He might as well have asked me to sign something. I would have demanded 20 percent of the cause of death, as well as some other clauses. I'm a daughter of lawyers. But when I heard that big kid speak to Merlin, I was filled with sorrow. And longing. I wanted to take the phone. I would have submitted to his voice, getting a few moments of paternal protection from it. Even Zoe Navon needs that kind of thing once in a while.

I rested my head on Rai's shoulder and followed Gili Levin with my eyes. She also received the Medal of the Gray Blanket and was standing limp-limbed, next to the dead cop, whose body was covered by another blanket. It was morning, and I could see her clear eyes, not looking at anything and looking at every little bit of the world.

There are fairy-tale princesses, and then there's Zoe Navon. But she has her moments, too. Because the phone rings in my pocket, and I inadvertently pull out the gun and give it to Rai, who's startled and tries to put the safety on, to unload it, but looks like a squirrel trying to solve a chess problem composed by the master José Raúl Capablanca. I put the safety on for him and then answer the phone. It's sweet Jonah Merlin.

He asks questions. I hold back. I don't always need to celebrate victories. I only ask him if it's definitely over, and he says yes, the murders are over.

Something inside of me is so light all of a sudden. I don't even want Carmela Tzedek to apologize anymore. I've won, and I don't need any losers. Sweet Jonah Merlin . . .

I look into the distance, searching for daylight and hoping that here in the desert it will be strong, superstrong, and suddenly I remember Bruno's words, the pillar of fire he saw on the rug in his room, the plenty that was released, and like shadow puppets I see before me the lines that a girl like Zoe Navon has no problem memorizing: "I have been telling you that everything is held back, tamed, walled in by boredom, unliberated! And now look at that flood, at that flowering, at that bliss . . . And I shed tears of happiness and helplessness."

That line—"and I shed tears of happiness and helplessness"—I don't get it, everything that happened here . . . all this stuff . . . What does it have to do with Bruno Schulz?

EPILOGUE

I first encountered Bruno Schulz when I happened upon his book *The Street of Crocodiles*, which had been translated into Hebrew as *The Cinnamon Shops*. I bought it as a gift I never ended up giving, and so the book spent a few months sitting on my bedside table, mine and not mine, waiting for the moment when I would decide to open it. I can't remember when and why I started reading it, but I remember the dripping: I dripped into a wondrous world. Story by story, Bruno Schulz's strange, shimmering writing pulled me in, as if the magnetic core of the world were calling to me. Then I reached the epilogue and learned the story of Schulz's life and death.

What is it about Bruno Schulz that won't leave me alone to this day? Certainly, the stories themselves are magical, but they are not the explanation. Neither is Bruno's curious personal story, dying as the miserable victim of a Nazi sadist—a painful, heartbreaking tale, enough to explain the fact that I've been dealing with Bruno for years, reading his stories over and over, each time as if for the first time, collecting every bit of information I could about his life, traveling to strange places to meet people who knew him, and most of all, getting emotional. Still getting emotional about everything that has to do with him.

What ties me to him? After years of asking this question, I've reached a conclusion: nothing. We differ in every possible way, and so it's hard to understand why, of all my favorite writers, of all the people whose life stories touched me, Bruno Schulz is the only one constantly fluttering within me. I followed him all the way to his hometown of Drohobych, located in what is today one of the less appealing parts of Ukraine, just to go to the places where he once walked. Just to see where he taught students who later terrorized him. Just to spend a few moments in the house where he wrote and on the spot where he was shot in the street.

For me, reading Schulz's stories is like drinking a contrast medium, the kind that doctors use to examine the inside of a body, or, in my case, the inside of my soul. The element in his stories that speaks to my most profound depths is his father. The relationship between a father and his son. For me, it's a simple story: I am lucky enough to have a wonderful father (I sometimes refer to him as the fire pillar of my life), who is one of the sanest people I know in this crazy world. For Bruno Schulz, things were a little different.

Schulz wrote mostly about his father, who died in 1915 but was lost to his son several years earlier; a kind, loving father who went out of his mind before the eyes of his oversensitive child. All of Schulz's writing is really a desperate attempt to adhere to the edict of honoring one's parents, a courageous attempt to turn the world inside out like a sock, so that everyone may know that his father was the biggest victor in this life. In each story, he fulfilled this edict anew, reinventing his father as a hero, a winner, the only man who lived a worthy life. In all his stories, he sent his father to dare and to break into pieces, presenting us with a man of rare bravery who knew he was destined to crash before he ever took off. (He always crashed as a result of contact with reality, even the lightest of contacts: the tickle of Adela the servant's finger, a change in the weather, any little thing.) In each story anew, Bruno stands before us, handing over his father as the one who at least tried, the one who drank from the goblet of life with all the bitterness and poison and sludge it contains, but drank nonetheless, unlike us—the petty bourgeoisie, clinging to our lives like snails on a mossy rock.

Over the years, I've written little essays about Bruno, things intended only for me, because the moment I begin discussing Bruno Schulz, I can't shut up. Bruno and Bruno and Bruno. And then, suddenly, this book: a serial killer, the terrible guilt of the innocent, endless sorrow . . .

What I mean to say is this: I've always known that one day I would write a book entirely devoted to Bruno's character, but I had no idea it would be this book, with Jonah Merlin and Zoe Navon and the Tel Aviv rain.

Bruno left us so little when he was murdered. And so much. Every word in his oeuvre releases a quiet spring that babbles slowly, an endless stream, creating stalagmites and stalactites for certain readers. More than seventy years after his murder, there isn't a year that doesn't see the publication, somewhere in the world, of a work of art inspired by the writing of Bruno Schulz.

I know nothing will help. Neither my words, nor the words of others, can grant Bruno Schulz even one more hour of life. We write about the dead and hope, at best, that what we write will prolong their memory a bit. But in the case of Schulz, it would be nice if something of all these words would ignite a storm, a change, a window into the world of the dead; and if he, shy, careful, nervously smoothing the edges of his coat, would peek into the land of the living once more.

He'd probably be hit by a car within five minutes.

Bruno didn't fit. He just didn't fit.

While he was alive, Bruno Schulz reduced his demands on life into a tiny crumb that wouldn't disturb a soul, and ever since his death he's become endless, spreading over the world, hidden, almost transparent, but forever existent, continuing to tell his stories through the paintbrushes and pens of other artists, turning a blind eye to his death.

ABOUT THE AUTHOR

Amir Gutfreund was born in Haifa in 1963. After studying applied mathematics at the Technion, he joined the Israeli Air Force, where he worked in the field of mathematical research. The author of five novels and a collection of short stories, he received the Buchman Prize from the Yad Vashem Institute in 2002, the Sapir Prize in 2003, the Sami Rohr Choice Award from the Jewish Book Council in 2007, and the Prime Minister's Award in 2012. Gutfreund lived with his family in the Galilee in northern Israel. In November 2015, at the age of fifty-two, he passed away after a brave battle with cancer.

ABOUT THE TRANSLATORS

Yardenne Greenspan has an MFA in fiction and translation from Columbia University. In 2011 she received the American Literary Translators Association Fellowship, and in 2014 she was a resident writer and translator at the Ledig House Writers Omi program. Her translation of *Some Day*, by Shemi Zarhin (New Vessel Press), was chosen for *World Literature Today*'s 2013 list of notable translations. Her full-length translations also include *Tel Aviv Noir*, edited by Etgar Keret and Assaf Gavron (Akashic Books), *Alexandrian Summer* by Yitzhak Gormezano Goren (New Vessel Press), and *The Secret Book of Kings* by Yochi Brandes (St. Martin's Press). Yardenne blogs for *Ploughshares* and served as *Asymptote Journal*'s editor-at-large of Israeli literature. Her writing and translations have appeared in the *New Yorker, Haaretz, Guernica, Asymptote,* the *Massachusetts Review,* and *Words Without Borders,* among other publications.

Evan Fallenberg is the author of the novels *Light Fell* (Soho Press, 2009) and *When We Danced on Water* (HarperCollins, 2011) and is a translator of Hebrew fiction, theater, and film. He has won or been shortlisted for many prizes, including an American Library Association Award for Literature, the PEN Translation Prize, and the *TLS* Risa Domb/Porjes Prize for Translation of Hebrew Literature. Fallenberg heads the literary translation and fiction programs at Bar-Ilan University and for five years was a guest faculty member of the MFA program in creative writing at City University of Hong Kong. The recipient of fellowships from the MacDowell Colony, the National Endowment for the Arts, Fondation Ledig-Rowohlt, and the Banff Centre for Arts and Creativity, Fallenberg is the founder and artistic director of Arabesque: An Arts & Residency Center in Old Acre.